No Goodbye

The rows between Mu... ...a long time. Now Mum ... trial separation, and thin... ...e again.

Greg, Lucy, Conor and ... are hurt, angry, worried, confused. They want their family to stay together. But what can they do about it?

Dad has little or no time to spend with the children. How will he cope with both a job and a home to run? Above all, when will Mum return?

Told from the point of view of each of the four children, this book explores the heartbreak, hope and determination of a family in crisis.

'Very authentic ... an honest book that many will identify with'
SUNDAY PRESS

'Full marks to the best-selling Marita'
BOOKS IRELAND

Special Merit Award to The O'Brien Press
from Reading Association of Ireland
'for exceptional care, skill and professionalism in publishing, resulting in a consistently high standard in all of the children's books published by The O'Brien Press'

MARITA CONLON-McKENNA

DUBLIN-BASED WRITER Marita Conlon-McKenna has won an International Reading Association Award (USA) for her novel on the Great Irish Famine, *Under the Hawthorn Tree*. She also won the Österreichischer Kinder- und Jugendbuchpreis (Austria), the Bisto Book of the Year Award (Ireland) and was nominated for Le Prix Litteraire Du Roman Pour Enfants (France). Her work has been translated into many languages, including Japanese, French, Dutch, German, Swedish, Italian, Danish.

BOOKS PUBLISHED

Under the Hawthorn Tree

Wildflower Girl

Fields of Home

Safe Harbour

The Blue Horse

In Deep Dark Wood

Little Star

No Goodbye

Marita Conlon-McKenna

THE O'BRIEN PRESS
DUBLIN

First published 1994 by The O'Brien Press Ltd.,
20 Victoria Road, Rathgar, Dublin 6, Ireland.
Tel. +353 1 4923333; Fax. +353 1 4922777;
e-mail: books@obrien.ie
website: www.obrien.ie
Reprinted 1995, 1998, 1999.

ISBN 0-86278-362-3

British Library Cataloguing-in-publication Data
Conlon-McKenna, Marita
No Goodbye
I. Title
823.914 [J]

4 5 6 7 8 9 10
99 00 01 02 03 04 05

The O'Brien Press receives
assistance from

The Arts Council
An Chomhairle Ealaíon

Typesetting, layout, editing, design: The O'Brien Press Ltd.
Cover separations: C&A Print Services Ltd., Dublin
Printing: The Guernsey Press Co. Ltd.

CONTENTS

The Fourth Week

The Fifth Week

The Sixth Week

Walkout

GREG – *Tuesday*

'She's gone!'

There's no screaming or shouting, no banging of doors, no cases flung in the hall, nothing dramatic like in films or on television to show that my Mum has walked out and left my Dad and the four of us. All there is is him, home early, sitting quietly in the kitchen, reading and re-reading the long folded pages of a letter Mum has left for him.

'I got a message in the office so I came home as early as I could,' Dad explains. 'Sit down all of you, I want to talk to you.'

An alarm bell begins to trigger inside my head as we all settle noisily at the kitchen table. Dad looks so strange, so serious.

'Where's Mum?' asks Lucy.

'That's what I have to talk to you about,' says Dad. He takes a deep breath. 'Your Mum has left, she's ... gone away, God knows where!'

It seems as if our kitchen has become very small, and the walls are tilting and falling in on us. And the next minute it is huge and empty and vast. One minute, two minutes pass and I'm still sitting on my pine chair in the same spot.

'This letter, it tries to explain why,' Dad's voice trails off, '... but I don't really understand it,' he continues, annoyed. 'Why would she do such a thing?'

Lucy and I stare at each other. Deep inside we both know why.

Conor and Grace jump up, push back their chairs and stampede out of the kitchen and off up the stairs. I can guess where they're going. But this is no big hide-and-seek game or treasure hunt.

'I checked already,' Dad tells us, his eyes hurt and full of confusion. The floorboards creak overhead, and the wardrobe doors slam and bang. The hunt is on. In about two minutes flat my younger brother and sister are back down again, both huffing and puffing and out of breath. Eyes huge.

'Mum's shoes are gone!' Conor yells, fear in his voice now.

'Her jacket and her handbag too,' adds Grace solemnly.

'The blue case is missing.'

'Her face cream, her hairbrush and the good perfume you gave her at Christmas, Daddy. It's all gone.' Grace makes it sound like a list of stuff some weird burglar had stolen from my parents' bedroom.

'But her nightdress is under her pillow, so ...' Conor points out.

'So?' says Dad.

'So, I suppose Mum will come back tonight,' Conor adds hopefully, but his voice breaks and he begins to sniffle.

Lucy stares at the kitchen dresser. All the hand-painted pottery and glassware Mum collects is displayed there. 'The photo is gone.'

We all turn around and suddenly notice the gap in front of the 'little hen' plates. There is, I mean there *was* a photo of us all, well us kids, the four of us on the beach in Brittas Bay last summer. It was a roasting hot day and we were all squinting into the sun, sunburned and freckled, when Mum took that photo.

'Why did she take the photo of us if ...?' Lucy begins to cry.

Then, wouldn't you know it, Grace copies her. At

six, Grace has got to be the biggest copycat I know. 'I want my Mummy back, I want her now!' she whines.

I'm never sure what to do when I see Grace cry. Usually if you give her a sweet or a biscuit she stops.

'Come on, now! It's not as bad as it seems. She'll probably be back in a day or two,' Dad says. He must be thick. It is definitely as bad as it seems, if not about ten times worse. 'Eat your chips,' he orders gruffly, 'they're getting cold.' How can the man eat take-away chicken and chips at a time like this?

'Greg,' he stares at me, 'eat up and pour out some more milk for Grace.' I read the challenge in his face and the hidden message: Pretend that we are a normal family, eating a normal meal, at a normal time. I stuff three big golden chips into my mouth and pretend. The others dry their tears and follow my good example and we eat those rotten chips till they are cold.

Lucy and Conor clear off the table and pack the dishwasher. I make Grace go up and get changed for bed. Dad is on the phone in the hall. I make a guess that he is telling Gran just what her daughter-in-law has done. His voice rises and falls but since

Grace wants me to read her a story about a school for little witches I can't really hear what he's saying. Now he's speaking so low he's whispering.

Nobody goes into the living room all night, or bothers to watch television. Lucy tries to do her homework, but her heart isn't in it.

'I'll give you a note for school tomorrow,' Dad promises.

I have maths, and science and German to do. I manage to get it all done. I definitely don't want a note! I don't want anyone at school to know about this disaster!

Supper is a huge plate of hot toast. It's real late by the time Lucy and Conor go to bed. Dad looks beat.

He's sitting on the couch watching the late-evening news. He spots me coming down the stairs. 'Come in and sit down, Greg!'

I sit and wait for him to tell me what's going on but he keeps on, by the way, watching planes and trains and politicians. I guess neither of us knows what to say.

'I don't know how I'm going to manage,' he says finally. 'I do love her,' he adds hesitantly.

'Yeah. I know, Dad.'

'She said it's to be a kind of trial separation,' he explains.

Then silence again. The empty space yawns between us. Mum is the talker of the family, my dad has always been the Quiet Man.

I wonder what exactly a 'trial separation' amounts to? Before I can ask, Dad says, 'How about a cup of coffee?'

'I'll get it,' I offer. I clatter about in the kitchen. This silence and stillness is driving me crazy.

By the time I bring in the coffee, his head is thrown back and he's snoring. Loud exhausted snores. I leave the mug down on the table near him. Poor Dad! He has driven all over the place today selling his stuff and what does he find when he gets home – a letter!

I wish he'd show me that letter. Maybe there's something in it for me.

He should have noticed more. The fighting has been going on in this house for a long time, like a little war with lots of sniper fire and every now and then a huge explosion. Worse still is when it goes quiet ... too quiet ... and Mum and Dad don't bother to talk or say a word to each other for hours or even days.

I saw all the warning signs, so why didn't he?

'Dad! Dad! I'm off to bed. Wake up a bit! There's your coffee.'

He half-stirs and wakes.

'Goodnight, Dad!'

The others are all asleep. I pull my quilt up to my neck and put on my walkman. The music uncoils inside my head. I know I'm too tired to listen – but it might stop me thinking.

Midnight Watch

LUCY – *Tuesday Night*

It's after midnight and really dark outside. Grace is snuffling in her sleep. I can't go to sleep.

I still can't believe it. Mum has actually left Dad. They fight a lot, but most mums and dads do that, don't they? For the last few days Dad has barely spoken to her. It's as if he was freezing her out, trying to pretend she was not in the house. And now he's got his wish. She isn't! The last time they had a really big row she said that some day he would push her too far and that there would be no going back. That day has come. What'll happen to us all?

The house is all locked up. Oh no! I bet Dad has put the chain on the door. What if Mum changes her mind and comes back and tries to sneak in quietly? She'll be locked out of her own house. I'd better go downstairs and check.

Yeah, all locked up – I knew it! Milk bottles on the doorstep, the chain across to keep burglars out. I undo the brass circle and let the gold links hang down heavily.

The living room is a mess. Dad always leaves the newspaper spread out on the carpet. The big arm-chair is all squashy and comfortable; I usually never get a chance to sit in it, and have all the cushions for myself. The fire is out and the heating is off. I pull my feet up under me to keep my legs warm and wriggle into the high back and sides, curling my toes in under the heavy softness, and hug the cushion to keep warm. I wonder where Mum is now?

Someone's coming! I can hear the pad of their feet, on the landing ... on the stairs ... in the hall ...

Greg pushes the door open.

'What the heck are you doing sitting here in the dark, Lucy?' he quizzes.

'It's not dark!' The small table lamp is on. 'Anyway, I'm thinking.'

Greg yawns and comes in to join me, lowering himself down in front of a non-existent fire, both of us prepared to keep vigil.

'I couldn't get to sleep either!' he says.

'Did Mum tell you anything about this, Greg?' I ask.

He shrugs.

'Is that a yes or a no?'

'Nope.' He sounds definite. 'What about you?'

I consider. 'No! Not really. But I knew she was upset. Do you think Mum is all right, Greg?'

'Probably ... I guess she's just had enough of rows and fighting,' he says flatly. 'She probably wanted to put a bit of distance between herself and Dad. Dad said it's a kind of trial separation. Maybe she needs time to think about whether they'll separate finally or something.' My big brother stares at me, watching for reaction. He knows me far too well.

'Maybe or maybe not. She'll come back,' I say, 'I know she will. Mum wouldn't walk out just like that and leave us. They probably just had another fight.' I'm trying to convince myself as well as Greg.

'Honestly, Lucy! You're so innocent. The statistics on marriage break-ups are sky high.'

I don't care about those facts and figures. This is *our* Mum and *our* Dad, not some stupid strangers! The goosepimples are erupting up all over my legs and arms and back. I snuggle deeper into the chair for comfort.

Conor suddenly appears, his hair standing on end. He must have sneaked down the stairs after Greg; he was probably listening to us at the door.

'You two gave me an awful fright,' he murmurs, 'I thought you were burglars! If Mum and Dad separate where will we live?' he continues immediately. 'Will Dad have to move out? Will we all have to move to a smaller house?' Conor asks question after question. You can tell by his thin face that he's all wound up.

'Why can't we stay here?' I can't stop myself getting upset, and tears roll down my face.

'They'll sell it!' Conor offers morosely.

'Look! Hang on! We don't know that or anything for sure yet,' Greg tells us.

I like living here, I like this house, I like this road, I like all these rooms.

'Listen, we'll probably be staying here,' reassures Greg.

'No way!' shouts Conor. 'They always sell the house, move out. Dad will probably end up living in an apartment ... there will be lawyers and everything will get split down the middle.' He's getting so excited that bits of spit fly out of his mouth.

I feel scared.

'Shut up, Conor!' warns Greg. 'You watch too much TV, that's your trouble! Our Mum and Dad aren't like that!'

'Yeah? Well, maybe if you watched it instead of spending all your time playing rugby you might know a bit more about what's going on,' Conor jeers.

'You little brat.' Greg is ready to hit him. Conor always seems to wind Greg up and drive him crazy.

'Stop it! The two of you, just stop it!' I try to break them up. 'Don't you think there's enough fighting going on in this house already? We'll all just have to try and join forces and get Mum and Dad back together again.'

'You're right, Lucy, this is our fight too,' says Greg.

But Conor is having none of it. He's too angry. 'Adults! What do *they* care about us? Why didn't Mum bother to tell us? No! She just upped and left us all. And the only thing *he's* worried about is that he'll be stuck here minding us! I know he is. They don't care about us — and I don't care about them!'

Greg and I both stare at him. Sometimes he's such a weird, angry kid.

'I'm going to bed!' he shouts and storms off up the stairs.

'It'll be up to us, Luce,' says Greg. 'Conor and Grace just won't understand.'

He's right. That's what big brothers and sisters are there for. I wish I had a big sister.

Greg yawns and gets to his feet. He squeezes my hand. He's getting really tall — soon he will pass Dad out.

'I'll stay up for a while,' I tell him.

'There's no point, Lucy. Come on, go to bed!'

'In a little while!'

He tiptoes back upstairs. I sit and wait till the pink dawn streaks the sky.

All in a Spin

GREG – *Wednesday*

The whole house is in a state of chaos and calamity, and yet Mum is gone less than twenty-four hours. I don't believe anyone got enough sleep last night, and we all look it. Dad's got bags under his eyes and Lucy's look sort of red and weepy.

Conor and Lucy are having a massive fight on the landing, over a pair of navy socks. Lucy wins the tug-of-war.

Then Conor begins to whine, 'My tracksuit top and my socks are missing!' expecting somebody else to go searching for them.

Our hot press is like a tumble-dryer in mid-spin, everything is all over the place. Anything Mum ironed last week will be all creased and crumpled by now, and it's every man for himself as we pull out the clothes we need.

'The wash basket is full,' I say, staring at Lucy.

'So!' she says.

'Well, *someone* had better do some washing!'

'SOMEONE! Well, which someone did you have in mind?' she replies sarcastically.

'You, of course! Lucy, come on, you must have watched Mum often enough to know what to do!'

'I've watched her for twelve years, I admit,' she snaps, 'but you've watched for over fourteen years, so you should *really* know!'

'Stop fighting, you two!' says Dad. He grabs the big wash basket and empties it out on the floor. 'Now, sort them into piles,' he orders. 'Coloureds and whites, I suppose,' he adds a little uncertainly.

Grace just stands there, naked, watching us all.

'Gracey! Go and get dressed!' I yell at her.

She looks at me with big sad blue eyes, and doesn't budge.

'Go easy on her, Greg. She's had a rough night. She doesn't understand what's going on, and she's scared,' whispers Lucy. 'I'll get her dressed in a few minutes, but she needs to have a bath first.'

Apparently when Lucy eventually went back up to bed last night, she discovered Grace had had an accident and peed all over herself, and then clambered into Lucy's bed, and was upset because Lucy wasn't there.

The stink off those wet sheets!

'Greg! Put those sheets and pyjamas of Grace's down in the washing machine and turn it on!' orders Dad.

'I will not,' I say. 'I'm not going into school smelling of that! Anyway, I'm not sure how to use the machine.'

Dad's got his good suit on, so he can't do it, and Conor has disappeared off to the loo.

'Leave them! I'll do it,' offers Lucy resignedly, 'but Grace is going to have her bath first!'

Grace climbs into a bath full of pink bubbles that Lucy has run for her, and is busy washing her Barbie doll's hair.

'Dad! You stand and watch her!' orders Lucy, as Dad tries to slink off downstairs to read the paper in peace. He stands over the bath watching Grace until Lucy is ready to dry and dress her.

When he comes downstairs I don't bother telling him about the damp patch on the sleeve of his suit where Grace splashed him. I'm sure he'll notice it soon enough.

Now, Grace won't eat her breakfast. Two bowls of Rice Krispies lie on the table in front of her.

'Too much milk,' she complains. 'Too soggy.'

Dad looks as if he could shake her. 'Come on, pet!' he pleads, 'be a good girl and eat up.'

Grace shakes her head and sticks out her bottom lip. 'No! No! No!' she screams. 'I want Mummy to do it!'

Lucy arrives dressed in her school uniform and takes in the situation at once.

'Ah! Goldilocks!' she says softly, while pouring out a fresh bowl and sprinkling sugar on the top. 'This bowl of porridge is too hot!' says Lucy dramatically. 'This bowl of porridge is too salty! ... And this little bowl of porridge is,' she pours the milk on as quick as lightning and shoves it under Grace's nose, 'just perfect.'

Grace plunges in her spoon and gobbles it all up.

Dad and I are stunned by this twelve-year-old psychologist. Lucy nibbles at the corner of her crusty brown bread nonchalantly.

Conor is sullen and quiet. He eats a bowl of cereal, and avoids looking at anyone.

Dad is trying to make turkey-roll sandwiches for us all. He forgets the lettuce and has to open them all and stick a bit of green in, before packing them again in the lunchboxes.

The postman comes and Conor runs out to bring in the letters. Just two bills. Nothing else. Nothing from Mum.

'I'm taking Grace to school today,' announces Dad, 'and Gran will collect her later and come back here for the rest of the day and cook dinner for us all.'

'That's just great!' mutters Conor. Gran is always on at him.

'She's helping us out, Conor, so be nice to her,' Dad warns. 'I'll have to ask Deirdre to help as well. We can't expect Gran to be here every day.' Deirdre lives across the road. She has a small baby of her own, and she sometimes minds Grace if Mum has to go somewhere.

The clock shows eight-thirty. I'll be late for the school bus. Grabbing my bag and lunchbox I race to the stop. Through the steamed-up windows I see Barry and Don and Niall. I pretend not to notice them and sit on a spare seat in the front and take out a book. If I get through today I'll be okay.

Little Girl Lost

GRACE – *Wednesday*

Granny came over to mind me again today.

She tried to make me happy and bought me an ice-cream cone on the way home from school.

We played five games of snakes and ladders, and I won three of them.

We made brown bread, and some buns. Then she had a little nap when she finished reading the paper.

I want Mummy to come back now, right now! I just want my own Mummy.

Mummy and Daddy have separated. Daddy told me about it. He said it means that Mummy is gone away for a little while. It's because they are always fighting.

Mummy still loves me and Lucy and Conor and Greg, but she just doesn't love Daddy as much any more.

Conor says she has gone away to think about it and to decide what's best for us all.

I wish Daddy had gone and Mummy had stayed to mind me.

Gran

GREG – *Wednesday*

By the time I get home from school, the late afternoon sun is slanting into the kitchen where my grandmother is busy slicing vegetables. I don't know what our family would do without Gran, she's always ready to come around when we need her.

I bite into a chunk of raw carrot.

'Well, Greg! How are you doing?' she gives me a tragic look. 'This is a terrible thing to do ... I don't know what's come over Vanessa. I had no idea ... We've been through so much together, good times and bad times, ups and downs, the four of you being born, starting school ... You know, your Mum was very good to me when your poor grandad was sick and dying. Why couldn't she have talked to me? Maybe I could have helped.'

Normally, Mum and Gran are really close, and when Mum went into hospital to have Grace, years ago, Gran came and stayed here and took over, and afterwards she used to come over a lot because Mum got that kind of baby depression thing. Dad always said it was Gran that got Mum smiling and back on her feet again.

'Your Mum is devoted to all of you. Why would she go off to London like this, leaving a good home and a lovely family? I just don't understand it. Poor Chris is in a state of shock!'

Gran's round face is flushed with annoyance and exertion and puzzlement as she chops away, decimating the carrots into tiny thin strips.

'All marriages have their rough patches, Greg, you know, that's nothing unusual. I know Chris has his faults, but you just don't throw away years ...'

I stare at the table. I can't stop the tears coming in my eyes. I wish she'd stop getting us both upset, talking about Mum like this. It's not going to do any good.

Gran lifts her grey-blond permed head to look at me, then wipes her hands on her apron and surprises me with a hug, warm and comforting and smelling of cologne.

'Don't mind me, Greg! I'm sorry for going on. This is probably just a storm that will blow over. Your mother will realise what she's missing, and come back home in a day or two.'

'Gran, I've a load of homework to do,' I tell her.

'Okay, Greg. I'll give you a shout when the dinner is ready.'

It's a relief to escape upstairs. My bedroom is cluttered and small. Dad set up a desk for studying. Above it are shelves with all my books and tapes. I change out of my uniform and sit down and spread out my books. What the hell do I care about the state of France during the revolution when my whole life and home are falling apart! Then a terrible thought crosses my mind: Gran might have to come and live with us and I might have to give up this room and share with Conor!

*   *   *

Dad is late as usual, so the four of us end up having dinner with Gran. The beef casserole is just great and there's a large tray of crispy roast potatoes to go with it.

Conor stares at Gran with narrow, jealous eyes when she sits down in Mum's chair. Lucy keeps staring at the back door as if any minute now Mum will walk in and catch her eating – she actually feels guilty!

My stomach is rumbling and Gran is delighted when I wolf down a huge plate of dinner.

'Going hungry never helped solve a problem,' she rambles on, cutting up another potato for Grace. 'I suppose I'd better put your Dad's dinner in the oven to keep it warm,' she adds.

'Mummy always has to do that!' puts in Grace, 'and she gives out about it too.'

It's almost eight when we hear the car door slam in the driveway. We're all watching TV. Dad appears in and nods to us all before heading into the kitchen with Gran. He doesn't come back for ages. Obviously he's getting a talking to. My grandmother is a lady with lots of opinions and she's not shy about sharing them all. I'd better rescue him.

'Hiya, Greg!' he says when I come into the kitchen. 'How was school? Everything okay?'

Gran leaves us alone.

'Fine, Dad. We've a rugby match on Saturday.'

The Junior Bs are not the best team but we're getting there. Once we practise and keep in good shape, there's always a chance of getting picked for the A team. Last year Barry's brother played in the semi-finals and finals when one of the A guys got a burst appendix. One man's bad luck is another man's good luck.

'How was your day, Dad?' I ask.

He shrugs his shoulders, takes off his jacket and flings it on the chair. 'Four chemists and a creamery, a surgery and two racing stables – the usual!'

Being a medical rep for a pharmaceutical company means Dad has to travel a lot. At the moment he's hawking the latest veterinary products. He sounds and looks tired out. It must be hell driving around trying to sell stuff with this kind of turmoil going on.

* * *

Grace won't go to bed for Gran, so Lucy is trying to coax her.

Conor is stuck with his homework. Usually Mum helps him and listens to his spellings. Dad does his best to give a hand, but he doesn't do it properly and Conor ends up flinging the book at him.

'Highly strung! Just like his mother,' mutters Gran. 'Chris, I have to go,' she says at last. 'I promised Marjorie I'd call over to finalise plans for our art group's annual trip.' She's busy buttoning up her jacket, then she fixes a silk scarf around her neck.

'Maybe I should cancel the trip?' She looks anxiously at Dad.

'Mum! Don't even think of it! We'll manage. Thanks for coming. I don't know what we'd all do without you,' Dad says.

'It's the least I could do.' She fusses, gives him a hug and says, 'I'll be round again tomorrow, but don't forget, Chris, Friday is my Meals On Wheels day, and I can't let the old people down.'

Dad nods, gives her a peck on the cheek and waves her off as she gets into her old Renault 4. Now it's just the five of us.

Secrets

LUCY – *Thursday*

Mrs O'Malley, my teacher, is talking to the class about Newgrange. We're going to go on our school tour there. She has photocopied pages with lists of things to look out for and Carrie is busy giving them out.

I just feel awful today. I can hardly hear what Mrs O'Malley's saying. There's a tickly lump in my throat, and my eyes keep filling up with tears. I can't help crying. I try to let my hair fall over my face a bit so nobody will see, and I kind of lean my face on my hand so I look like I'm really concentrating. I need to blow my nose.

Brenda, who sits next to me, is staring ahead. It's funny, but when you think of someone, they suddenly feel it, and she turns around to me, then reaches into her schoolbag, and passes me a small packet of tissues. She always has a supply, as her hayfever starts around this time of year. I dab my eyes and blow my nose quietly.

Jill swings around and notices me. 'What's wrong?' she whispers.

I close my eyes and don't answer. I didn't tell anyone yesterday. But today I just can't keep up the pretense that everything's normal.

Mrs O'Malley stops talking, looks down towards us and then decides to continue.

It's so hard to think about school things and visiting ancient burial sites, when all I keep thinking about is home, and Mum and Dad, and what's going to happen. How long does a trial separation go on, and what happens then? Huge tears push their way out and I make this strange gulping sound when I try to swallow.

Brenda is talking to me. 'Lucy! Lucy!'

Mrs O'Malley stops. 'Brenda Brophy! What's going on down there?'

'It's Lucy, Miss. She's crying.'

'What's the matter?' the teacher asks, all concerned now. 'Lucy Dolphin, are you feeling all right?'

I'm afraid to say even one tiny word, because if I do, I know I'll end up bawling like a big cry-baby.

Brenda seems to understand. 'She's not feeling well, Miss!' she lies. 'Maybe she might get sick.'

Mrs O'Malley squints down towards me. Like all teachers, she just hates it when someone throws up in the classroom, and they have to clean it up and open all the windows and get disinfectant to get rid of the smell.

'Then, take her out, Brenda, quickly now, take her down to the infirmary.'

Brenda pushes back her chair and stands up and manages to get me out the classroom door. All the others are watching me.

Brenda walks beside me down the wide sunny corridor. She's waiting for me to tell her what's going on, but at the moment I just feel too miserable to talk.

The infirmary is really just a small little room with a kind of couch-bed in it and a blanket and pillows, and two armchairs. The teachers also use it for storing wall charts for class work. There's a big first-aid poster stuck on the wall telling you what to do in emergencies, like choking or falling or getting stung.

One of the second-class girls is already there, sitting on a chair with a woolly hat on her head. I remember getting that hat on when I was younger – it's a special knitted blue bee-hive hat with flaps for people with sore ears. It's meant to keep your ears warm and make you feel better. Sister Catherine is reading the girl a story. She looks up questioningly when she spots Brenda and me.

'Mrs O'Malley sent us down,' explains Brenda, 'Lucy isn't well. She's upset.'

Sister Catherine peers at me anxiously, and reaches to a shelf for a white plastic bowl, which she hands me.

'Brenda, you may go back to class now. Thank you, I'll look after Lucy.'

Brenda nods. 'See you later, Lucy!' she calls back to me as she heads off.

Sister Catherine shoves a thermometer into my mouth. I already know it's going to read normal.

She takes it out and glances at the silver line. 'No fever anyway! Would you like me to phone your mother, Lucy?'

'No!' I shake my head. 'She's out!' I tell her. It's only a half-lie.

'Well, maybe if you have a rest there for a while, you may feel a bit better soon!' She's trying to be tactful and doesn't ask why my eyes are all red and weepy. She potters around and lets me be.

The other girl looks ghastly pale, and after about twenty minutes her mother arrives to collect her.

* * *

It's break-time and Sister Catherine goes to join the rest of the staff for a cup of tea. I am to ring the little brass hand-bell if I need her.

Brenda and Jill knock on the door, and see that I'm on my own.

'The coast is clear,' Jill laughs. 'Is it okay for us to come in?'

I wish they had gone out into the yard with the rest of the class and left me alone.

'Did you get sick?' asks Jill. Honestly, she's a real

curiosity box, even if she is one of my best friends.

'No!'

'That's good anyway,' says Brenda, moving over and sitting on the edge of the couch. 'Is your Mum coming to get you?'

'No! She's out ... She's not around!'

'Oh!'

'Actually ...' I make up my mind to tell them, 'she's gone away.' I hate bottling things up, keeping secrets. 'My Mum has left my Dad, left all of us. They've split up!'

They are both totally silent and I can tell they haven't a clue what to say to me.

'When did she go?' asks Brenda.

'Tuesday. She left a letter. It's a sort of trial separation,' I explain.

'How long is she gone for?' asks Jill.

'I don't know. My Dad won't say!'

'Does she have a boyfriend? Has she met someone else?' Jill asks.

It's weird, but I hadn't even thought of that. I shake my head. 'No, definitely not.'

'Are they going to get a divorce?' Brenda's voice is full of concern.

'No, Brenda! I don't think so! Look, I just don't know yet. All I know at the moment is that my Mum is not at home, and that none of us are sure what the hell is going to happen.' I'm almost shouting at them.

'No wonder you were crying,' Brenda says softly. 'You must miss her so much!'

I close my eyes because I feel like crying again.

Brenda puts her arm round my shoulder. 'It's all right, Luce! Jill and I understand, don't we, Jill?'

Jill is standing there, twirling a piece of her hair round her finger, not sure what to make of it all. Her Mum and Dad never have rows or fights.

'It happens to lots of people,' Brenda tries to reassure me. 'Sure my Mum and Dad are always on at each other. Look at Orla, her parents separated when she was a baby, and you know about Caitriona, her Dad is living down in Wicklow with his new girlfriend.'

'Yeah!' adds Jill, 'and don't forget Carrie, the new girl!' We all know about Carrie and her Mum moving back to Ireland, and her Dad who still lives in New Jersey, with his new wife and Carrie's two little half-brothers. She's always telling us stories about her life in America, and the house and the school and the friends that she had to leave behind when her Mum and Dad got divorced.

I hope that doesn't happen to me.

'Listen, Lucy! We're your friends. Whatever happens with your parents, we're your best buddies!' Brenda is looking right at me. She is my best friend in the whole world. Her face is freckled, she has blue-grey eyes and her brown hair is tied back in a pony-tail. Next year, she has to get 'train-tracks' on her teeth, as her top ones stick out too much. Eventually I'll be pretty, she keeps saying, but I like her just the way she is.

'Yes,' Jill agrees. 'We'll be around,' she offers hesitantly. Sometimes Jill is so self-centred, all she worries about is being top of the class and getting high marks. Already she's obsessed with going to college. Brenda and I are always trying to get her to relax about school.

'Thanks!' I mumble.

They both give me a sort of a hug, and we cling together, with me sniffling and both of them nearly crying too.

Sister Catherine walks in. 'What's going on, girls?

What are the two of you doing down here when class is due to start?'

I blush. It's my fault. 'I'm feeling a lot better, Sister, and they came down to take me back to class.'

'Are you sure, Lucy?'

'Yes, Sister! Honestly! I feel a whole lot better now!'

Hare and Hounds

CONOR – *Thursday*

'Conor Dolphin, stand up! Spell the word "furniture",' says Miss Boland.

I stare down at the floor.

'Did you hear me, Conor?'

My shoes are dusty, they need a good polish.

'Well! Let's try another word from your word-list: "factory".'

I still don't know it. John is trying to whisper something to give me a hint, but I can't hear him.

'Conor, did you learn any of the words from this week's list?'

'I tried, Miss Boland.' I like my teacher. Her hair

is the same colour as my sister Grace's. She smells of flowers.

'Did you do any of your homework last night? Your workbook hasn't been handed up yet.'

'I forgot, Miss!'

Dad gave me a letter for her but I hid it in the zip pocket of my schoolbag. He said it would explain things.

'Oh Conor! What am I going to do with you!'

I don't answer her.

'All right, just sit down, Conor. Pay attention!'

Miss Boland moves on to someone else. She keeps on talking. I like the sound of her voice. It reminds me of my Mum. Mum promised me that she would always be there to help me. Every night just before tea-time, Mum helped me with my homework. We did my reading book, so I'd know what was coming the next day. The other kids think it's real easy to read. But I seem to keep on making mistakes or saying the wrong word. Mum never got cross the way Dad or Greg or Lucy do. She just smiled and sat right up close beside me, and I could feel her breath as we made the word-sounds.

'Some people take to swimming like fish,' Mum

used to tell me, 'while others have to have rubber rings and armbands and floats and lots of lessons before they can make it across to the far side of the pool. But remember, once they do that, in no time they can swim like fishes too.' That's what she told me. We would do my word list again and again until I knew it real well. If anyone came in, Mum would say: 'Out! It's Conor's time.'

She lied and broke her promise. I don't know who's going to help me now. Dad is too busy.

The bell will sound real soon, then it'll be break time and we can all go out to the yard. The school door opening and the rush of air in my face and the chance to run, that's what I love.

Gary and the rest of the class say that I'm the fastest racer in our yard. They try to beat me, but almost always I win.

'Hare and Hounds!' yells Gary.

That's the game we'll play today. The schoolyard is noisy and crowded. I'm the hare. Right around the yard, down as far as the school gate, over the swampy wet grass, back through the teachers' car-park, then up to where we play football. The goalpost is my home – I mean the hare's den.

One. Two. Three ...

I start to run. I have to scan my path ahead to make sure no small kids are in the way because they really slow you down. Three girls playing hopscotch, I'll go round them. The last few days it's been raining a lot, so the grass will be extra slippy.

Seven. Eight. Nine ...

Check the cars. Is there somewhere for me to hide? I must try to build up my pace.

Ten.

Ready or not, here come the hounds. There are seven of them. One or two are real fast.

I can feel my breath, it's getting louder. My legs feel like they are getting longer. My heart is pumping.

The hounds are miles away, maybe with the wind they won't be able to get the scent. I sniff the wind. I run ...

Today I feel scared. Maybe – maybe today is the day the hounds will get me. Some stupid kid runs out in front of me, I almost knock into her. I have to try and remember where I am.

The hounds are gaining. I can hear them.

'Yahoo! Yahoo!' Gary and Ian shouting. I have to run faster. They're gaining on me. The grass is slippery. I have to steady myself as I reach the tarmac, and begin to weave through the cars. No chance to hide as the hounds are too close. The goalpost is still far off in the distance. My head and neck are sweaty and the back of my throat hurts. I can hear the pounding of their feet as they get closer. I zig-zag like crazy. I must try to fool them if I am to reach the goal ...

'Gottcha! Gottcha!'

Gary grabs me first and pulls me on to the short grass. The ground is hard. Ian and Pat and the rest of the hounds all crowd around me. I try to laugh and pretend I don't care.

'The fast pack!' shouts Tommy O'Dowd. He squeezes my arm real hard so it hurts. Inside I feel shaky and shivery. I lost.

The teacher is shouting at us all. 'Get off that wet grass, boys!'

We all get up and start to move back down towards her. The others push ahead of me. John walks near me. He's a slow hound, because if he runs too fast he gets asthma. The sound of the bell fills the air and we all troop back inside.

I go to the cloakroom and soap my hands and

splash cold water on my face. By the time I get to class they should all be sitting down. Even from outside the door I can hear them: 'Can't read, can't run ... going to have to get a gun ... and shoot him!'

They all shout it louder when I come in. Gary is shouting the loudest. I hate him. I make like I'm going to cry and sit down and then just as I get beside his desk, I grab him by his jumper and give him a thump.

'Miss! Miss!' he screams. He isn't hurt that bad, otherwise my hand would be sore too.

'What is going on?' Miss Boland has just come in the door and is beside us in a second.

'He's not just stupid, Miss. He's crazy too!' Gary shouts.

I get that shaky, shivery feeling all over again. 'They were saying bad things about me,' I try to tell her.

'That's not fair,' she says, 'but it's not fair to hit someone either.'

Miss Boland makes us both shake hands and act like we're friends.

I wish school was over. I wish I was home. Most of all I wish Mum was there.

Big Brother

GREG – *Friday*

'Look, Dad, I'm not Mary Poppins!'

'Greg, I'm asking you to do me a favour. Missing one afternoon of rugby practice – is that too much to ask your son? It's only the B team anyway!' Dad shouts.

'Yeah! And if I don't practise, I'll end up on the C team for all you care.'

'Honestly, Greg, I wouldn't ask you, only this is a crisis. Your Gran can't come over. And Deirdre has to go to the dentist. It's one half-day – just collect Grace from school, and mind her for the rest of the afternoon,' he pleads.

'I'm not a nanny!'

Suddenly Dad smiles and gives me a big bear-hug. 'Come on! It won't kill you to spend an afternoon with your little sister. Bring her to the shops, or to the park if you want to.'

No way. Does Dad think I'm going to be seen walking around the place like a right sissy?

'It's a bit cold out, Dad. Grace is probably better off staying in.'

'You won't forget!' he calls after me.

*   *   *

The rugby coach didn't believe me, I could tell. 'Flu ... well, suspected 'flu. I know how lame an excuse it is. I look too healthy and well. A sprain would have been better, or even an ingrown toenail!

The tree-lined avenue that leads up to our school is flanked by the rubgy pitches. The Bs are all starting to line out and I can feel their stares as I shuffle past them in my jacket. I turn up the collar so it almost touches the end of my nose as I near the field where the seniors are busy warming up. They ignore me anyway. I have to walk slowly as I am meant to be sick.

Once outside the school gates I begin to jog. It's only about eight minutes to Belville Road, where Grace goes to the small primary school attached to the convent.

All the mothers stare at me. One lady in a denim jacket, her thick blond hair in a pony-tail, pushes her way forwards with a baby in a buggy until she is right beside me.

'How is Vanessa? You're her eldest boy, aren't you? Is she okay? I haven't seen her for a few days.'

Wouldn't you know it. *Someone* just had to be nosey.

'She's fine, just fine,' I lie.

'Nothing the matter at home is there?' she persists.

I shake my head in denial.

'Well, I just thought that ... I was worried about Vanessa.'

'No! Everything is fine, honestly. I'll tell her you said hello ...'

'Roz,' she adds.

Her baby is busy trying to climb out of the buggy, and she bends down to distract him. We all stand in a line outside the glossy, yellow-painted door. They are singing inside. Through the open window I can see all kinds of art and craftwork pinned on the wall. A mobile of paper butterflies dances and twirls as soon as the teacher opens the door. Talk about a push. They pile out worse than any rugby scrum.

No sign of Grace. I decide to go in and get her. I glance along the small tables, and there, sitting in the dappled sunlight, is Grace. She doesn't see me, as she's far too busy chatting to the little girl beside her. It's funny, but I never realised just how pretty Grace is.

She spots me and stands up, pushing her chair back gently. Then she picks up her pink schoolbag. 'Susie! That's my big brother Greg,' she says proudly.

Every head seems to turn and stare at me.

'Come on, Grace! Hurry up!'

We set off. At the first corner, Grace stands rigid, waiting.

'Come on!' I urge her. 'What's up?'

'You've got to hold my hand. Look, there's traffic.' She waves her hand towards the bumper-to-bumper cars driving along the main road. So, I don't know the rules!

We walk slowly along hand-in-hand. She chatters on about jigsaws and counters and numberbeads and what Susie had for lunch, until we reach home and the path up to our front door. She stops outside the door.

'Ring the bell!' she orders.

'It's no use,' I try to explain to her gently.

'Ring the bell!' she insists. 'Mummy will answer.'

'Look, Grace, nobody will answer. But I have the key.'

She cocks her neat, pointy little face to one side, almost like a dog, not sure whether to trust me or not.

I try to distract her. 'What'll we have for lunch today, Princess?'

'Food,' she mutters.

The minute the door opens she scampers in and flings her jacket and schoolbag in the hall. First she heads for the kitchen, then the living room and the dining room, even the toilet, before heading up the stairs. The house seems awful quiet and still. Usually by the time I get home the others are here.

Poor kid! Coming in to this every day. She trots around from bedroom to bedroom like a little hound sniffing and searching. I go to my room and sit on my bed and wait till she's finished her search. At last her sad face peeps in at me.

Deep inside I feel so angry. Angry for her and, I guess, a bit for myself.

'Not here,' she sobs.

'Yeah! I know, Princess.' I need to distract her. 'Would you like to look at my cars?'

She dries her eyes and nods half-heartedly.

The collection started when I was a kid of six. Dad

brought me back a vintage Rolls Royce and a Jaguar from a trip to London. Bit by bit it was added to. My grandad used to love it, and added a car every year for my birthday and for Christmas, right up to the time he died.

I take them all down from the overhead shelf that edges my whole room, and lay them on the carpet for her. She crouches down and picks out two to race, just like I used to. The gold glittery ones she hides behind my wastepaper bin.

'Hey, Grace, don't go hiding any of them. You're not allowed to take them to school. Come on, Princess, let's eat!'

Toasted cheese sandwiches – not very exciting, but Grace seems to like them. The cupboard is pretty bare. Upstairs in my room I have two cans of Coke hidden and I bring them down. Grace sucks on the red straw I found and blows bubbles in hers.

The afternoon stretches on. I'm not sure what you're supposed to do to amuse an energetic six-year-old. Although it's fairly cold out, the afternoon is bright. Grace leans against the window, watching me watching her. What does Mum do?

*   *   *

An hour in the park and already I'm exhausted. Rugby is a doddle compared to this. We use the stale bread that was going mouldy in the breadbin to feed the ducks. I pulled off all the green bits because Grace thinks they would poison the birds. She keeps standing too near the edge, trying to talk duck language; every few seconds she'll nibble a bit of the old bread herself, so the ducks will know how nice it is! There's a small playground down behind the tennis courts, and I have to push her about a hundred times on the swing. Up on the deserted bandstand she does a bit of ballet and her impression of Irish dancing. Two old ladies stop and sit down on the park bench to watch her, and I have to clap along with them when she bows at the end. Finally – *finally*, she agrees to come home.

'My legs are too tired to walk, Greg!'

Any wonder! I have to give her a piggy-back then. And wouldn't you know it, just when we reach the crossroads at the bottom of our road we bump into three guys from school.

'Hiya, Greg!' Barry Brady is on my team. 'You missed a good practice. I scored a try. New job?' he adds sarcastically.

'I had to babysit my sister, my Mum's away,' I explain.

Fergus Ryan takes over. He comes over and shakes Grace's hand, and she beams at him. That guy has a way with girls! It's just incredible, every girl in our area seems to fancy him.

'She's six,' I jeer at him.

'I know,' he tells me. 'She's great buddies with my kid sister, Aoife. Hey, Greg, how're things at home? It must be hard on everyone.'

'We're doing fine!' I tell him. 'Look, I've got to get home. I'll see you tomorrow.'

I trot off around the corner with Grace bouncing on my back. The three of them stand there looking after us. Everybody must know about Mum and Dad at this stage. We must be the talk of the neighbourhood.

The Supermarket

LUCY – Saturday

The supermarket is heaving with people. We should have been here at least an hour and a half ago.

'Dad! You push the trolley and I'll get the groceries,' I boss him.

Honestly, my Dad is over forty years of age and you would swear he had never set foot in a supermarket before. He doesn't seem to know where to start.

'Dad! Head for the frozen stuff – it's real easy to cook!' Greg says, and starts to march on ahead of us.

I try to picture Mum doing the weekly shop. 'No! Go to the fresh fruit and vegetables first!' I point Dad in that direction.

'We don't need that stuff,' moans Greg.

'Yes we do, or would you rather be all covered in spots and pimples?'

'Okay, okay, Luce! Just get some apples then.'

Dad is busy stuffing a plastic bag with green grapes. Mum usually only gets a tiny bunch, as they're so expensive. Next I stand in front of the vegetables. It looks like a big market stall. The guy has just sprayed all the vegetables with water so they look fresh and dewy and just picked.

'Dad, what'll we get?'

He just stares.

I try again. 'Dad, what meals will we be having?'

'When?'

'Next week.'

'Something fairly easy,' he says at last. 'And I was thinking maybe we'd eat out some days or get take-aways. Listen, Lucy, you pick out what you think is best. Gran can get more shopping during the week.' Dad thinks Gran is going to end up doing our shopping. That's just not fair.

We should have made a list like Mum always does, and some kind of meal plan. But it's too late now. Dad just lets us buy what we want. Given a free hand we all end up picking out our favourite food.

Dad drifts off among the Saturday shoppers and is busy sampling sausages, cheese, a new kind of curry sauce. I find him drinking a little plastic cup of wine, with a lady wearing a T-shirt in the colours of the French flag. She ignores the pensioners rambling by hoping for a little taste, and is busy chatting to Dad.

'We're nearly finished, Dad.'

Slightly embarrassed, he follows me. By the time we reach the checkout the trolley is stacked high.

Dad starts to put the groceries out, and in seconds manages to run our items in with the lady ahead of us. His mind just isn't on it.

'I didn't get frozen burgers!' she objects. 'That's not

my canned soup!' There's terrible confusion. The checkout girl is trying to stop giggling, and I feel as if the whole shop is staring at us. I just want to get out of there – quick! Dad gets a big shock when he sees how much all that food costs.

The minute we get home, Dad slumps on the sofa and has a mug of coffee. He leaves us to unpack.

Home Truths

LUCY – Saturday

While we're putting the shopping away the phone rings.

'Lucy, answer that!' calls Dad.

As soon as I pick it up, I know who it is. 'Hi, Lucy! How are you, pet?'

'Fine, Mum.' Imagine saying such a stupid thing. I want to say 'awful'. 'We've just come in from doing the groceries, and we're putting it all away.'

Dad sits still, pretending to read the newspaper.

'Honestly, Luce! You're great. I don't know what I'd do without you.'

But you *are* doing without me, is what I long to

say. 'Where are you, Mum?'

There is a silence. Dad has put down the paper, and he and Greg come right up beside me. I ask her again.

'I'm in London, pet, staying with Aunt Mary. I'm sorry I went so suddenly, Lucy. I feel really ashamed ... But if I didn't leave then I ... I mightn't have had the courage ... I needed to get away for a while and have a good think about everything that's happening between your Dad and me. I must give some proper consideration to this separation thing, and see if it's best for everyone. At home I just couldn't think straight. It felt like I was drowning bit by bit. I don't know if you can understand ...'

'It's all right, Mum!'

'Thanks, Lucy. How are the others?'

'They're all right, I suppose.'

'Are they?' She sounds kind of disappointed.

'Mum, Grace is upset. She's started to wet the bed again. And Conor is being real moody.'

Dad is glaring at me. Greg tries to pull the phone off me.

'Mum, the others want to talk to you too.'

'Wait! Before I go, pet – just don't let them take advantage of you.'

'Mum! When are you coming back?' I plead.

'I'm not sure yet, Lucy. There are so many things to sort out first.'

Greg grabs the phone. I run out to the hall, and shout up the stairs to Conor and Grace. 'Come down quickly! Mum is on the phone from London.'

They're in the middle of playing some game. Grace comes flying down the stairs so fast she almost falls. 'Where is she?'

'On the phone.'

'Will we see her tomorrow?'

I avoid telling her. 'Hurry up, Grace. Mum wants to talk to you. Conor! Conor! Come on down quick!'

No sound. I race up the stairs as fast as I can. Conor is staring out his bedroom window.

'Didn't you hear me? Mum is on the phone from London. She wants to talk to you.'

He doesn't budge. 'Well, I don't want to talk to her.'

His face is trying to be hard, but from the pain in his eyes, I know he's too hurt to talk to her. He picks up a transformer and begins to play with it, locking me out too.

By the time I get back downstairs, Grace is standing on the kitchen chair and singing a song she's learnt in school, as if Mum was here in the kitchen with her. Gabbling on and on.

Dad is waiting for his turn. He's real nervous. I suppose he doesn't know what to say. 'Where's Conor?' he demands.

I tell him.

'Bye, bye, Mummy! I love you too, Mummy ... kiss, kiss!' Grace's blue eyes are shining when Dad finally takes the phone from her.

'Vanessa.' He coughs and sounds hesitant. 'They're all okay. No! Conor won't talk to you. Well ... I'm trying ... I'm doing my best.'

Greg and I are dying to stay and listen, but Dad gestures to us to get out of the kitchen.

We sit at the bottom of the stairs in the hall. The old grandfather clock that Mum's aunt left her when she died ticks away in the silence of our long, narrow hall. Mum told me she used to hide in it when she was a small girl – her secret place in her Aunt Louise's old seaside house.

Dad's voice is getting louder. I can't believe it. They're having a row! *Now*! After all ...

'Totally irresponsible ... Self-centred! ... I will *not* call it a day!'

These words are not the words we'd hoped to hear.

Suddenly Dad stops talking and slams down the phone. He swears, then pulls open the door. Maybe he knew we'd be waiting here. He climbs in between Greg and me, pulling Grace onto his lap.

'Is it bad?' I ask, half-afraid. He won't answer. 'Are you really going to split up?' I persist. I *must* know.

Dad puts his arms around the three of us. 'I don't know, Lucy. Honestly, I just don't know. Your mother says this is a trial separation. She wants to see how we get on without each other. It's funny how some people can't live together, and yet they can't live apart either. Maybe Vanessa and I are like that!'

'But that means you *are* going to separate!' I say. I'm angry now.

'No, young lady! Hold your horses! No one is going to push me into anything that quick – anyway this is between your Mum and me.'

'No it isn't, Dad,' says Greg. 'This affects us all. We must know what's happening. We're not babies any more!'

'We're a family and we want to stay together,' I say.

'Come on! Give your old Dad a hug,' he begs us.

We all pounce on him, and let him know that we do care. Grace squeezes him so tightly, she nearly strangles him.

Conor is up on the landing. He looks down at us all, then he just turns and runs back into his bedroom and bangs the door.

Daddy's Girl

LUCY – *Monday*

It has been raining almost all day, and I got soaking wet on my way home from school. My hair is like rats' tails and my nose is all red at the tip because I'm getting a cold.

I've washed and peeled a big bag of potatoes and bits of their muddy skins are still clinging to the sink and taps. Now they're boiling away. Mince meat is frying in the pan, with some chopped up onions. I'm not mad about onions so there's only about half the amount Mum would use. The tomato sauce will give it a good flavour. The raindrops slide down the kitchen window which is all steamed up.

'Hi, Luce! What are you doing?' Dad's home early.

'I'm getting the dinner, Dad. We can't live on frozen pizza and chips for ever you know!'

'Hmmm! this tastes good,' he says, dipping his finger in the mince mixture.

'Some is for tonight, and the rest we can freeze for later.'

He looks at the freezer packs that I've left on the table.

'You are a very organised young lady,' he compliments me, making me blush. 'But you know, Lucy, you don't have to do all this. I appreciate it, we all do, but honestly, pet, no one is expecting you to take over from your Mum.'

The potatoes are well cooked and need draining. The saucepan is so hot and heavy, I can just about lift it, but the steamy liquid gushes out at me, as I try to strain it into the sink.

'Here, let me do that!' Dad fusses over me, almost scalding himself in the process.

The sink needs cleaning and so does the cooker – there's so much to be done. I can't help tears coming into my eyes.

'Are you okay, pet?' Dad asks, slipping his arm round my shoulder. 'I know it's really hard for you, Luce ...'

'Oh, Dad! It's just that I miss Mum so much ...'

'Of course you do, pet. And you're doing too much – trying to cook, mind Grace, get us all organised.

We'll just have to find some other way.'

'It's not just that ... I miss Mum the whole time. I keep thinking about her. I've no one to talk to. Mum is my very best friend.'

'Mine too!' he mumbles.

It's funny, but I hadn't thought about that. Sometimes, when things were going well, Mum and Dad would sit up half the night chatting. About films they had seen. Their old schooldays. Politics and what they would do if they were members of the government. Places they would visit when they had enough money. Poor old Dad!

'You must be dead lonely too, Dad.'

He doesn't answer me.

'When you and Mum got married ... you really loved each other then, didn't you? Why did it change?' I ask.

'I don't know, Lucy. Your Mum and I still love each other in our own way, but as you get older and busier things change, unfortunately not always for the better,' he confides.

'Was it because of us?'

'Lucy!' His voice is hurt. 'Never, ever, think that! Having the four of you was the best thing your Mum and I ever did. We may have messed up other things, but the four of you ...'

'But, Dad, if you and Mum still care about one another, why are you always fighting and hurting each other? Why do you stop talking to her sometimes?'

Dad doesn't know what to say. 'I have no answer, Lucy,' he stutters finally. 'I guess that's our problem, the reason Vanessa is in London and I'm here.' He won't tell me any more.

The meat is simmering in the brownish-red gravy. It'll dry out soon.

'Dad! I'd better start putting the dinner out.'

'Listen, Lucy! You're a great girl! If we pull together we'll get through this.'

The table needs setting, and I'm counting out the knives and forks, and listening to Dad at the same time. He kisses the top of my head.

'Is the dinner ready yet?' shouts Conor, running in. 'I'm starving!'

It seems to me that some people in this family have to pull a lot harder than others!

Promises

CONOR – *Monday*

Dad comes in from work and just sits down waiting for Lucy to put the dinner out on the table. He is reading a book, and never even bothers to glance up or say anything to me!

'Thanks, Dad!'

That gets his attention.

'Thanks for what, Conor?'

'Thanks for nothing! For forgetting to collect me from school today and take me to the dentist.'

He shifts uneasily in his chair. 'The dentist?'

'Yeah! You know I had to go to Mr Gibson at twelve o'clock today and you forgot about it!'

'I had an important meeting, son, and it just slipped my mind.'

'It's not fair, the way anything to do with me just doesn't matter!'

'I wasn't able –'

'I'm left standing like a right dork waiting for you for half an hour at the main door, with all the others passing by me, and in the end the headmaster sent me back to class because he didn't believe I was meant to be going to the dentist!'

'Look, Conor! I'm really sorry. I'll phone the school tomorrow, and I'll re-book the dental appointment.'

'You always forget things to do with us. There is a board up there.' I jam my fingers on our kitchen pinboard, and the calendar beside it. 'Mum wrote up all our important days and times and appointments on it. Why don't you just look at it!'

Dad gets up and peers at all the dates and school lists. He begins to unpin them and lifts the calendar off its hook. I think for a moment that he's going to tear them up and throw them in the bin. Lucy is standing with an armful of plates, watching him.

'What are you doing?' I demand.

'I'm going to take them into the office and photo-copy the whole damned lot of them, then I'll have my own set,' he says, and turning to look at me, he adds, 'and I promise I won't forget you or let you down again, Conor.'

For some strange reason I believe he means it and will keep his promise.

The Monster

GRACE – *Tuesday Night*

My room is dark, dark, dark.

There is a monster. I know he's here again. The monster pricks up his big furry ears to listen to me. His huge white and green eyes are watching me.

I pull my rabbit close up beside me. I hope that the monster prefers rabbits.

Mummy! My Mummy will come and open the wardrobe door and tell him Go away, and Get lost. She will search under my quilt and behind the curtains. She will put on my light, and frighten him away, and then stay with me.

My Mummy will come. I want her now.

Mummeeee!

I am so hot and scratchy.

Mummeee! I want my Mummeee!

Someone is standing in the doorway.

It's only my Daddy!

Night Duty

GREG – *Tuesday Night*

'Dad, I think you'd better get the doctor!'

This is crazy. It's four-thirty in the morning, and my eyes are bleary. We've been awake half the night, and Grace just keeps on and on crying. Lucy took her temperature and it's high. She's hot and flushed and confused. She keeps crying for Mum, and flings her dolls and teddy and the white rabbit on the floor. Her hair and face are all sweaty.

'Come on, Gracey, Daddy's here,' he keeps saying to her.

She lands him a mighty kick in the stomach. 'I want my Mummy! I want my Mummy!' she screams.

Lucy is frantic downstairs, searching the bookshelf in the kitchen for the *Family First Aid* book.

'Gracey, will I tell you a story?' I plead. Anything to pacify her and get her to calm down.

She swivels her wild, dilated eyes to look at me, and I see the hot, raging face of a stranger staring at me.

Dad runs into the bathroom and gets a wet facecloth to try to cool her down.

'Now, Grace, this will help you!' Dad does his best to make his voice soft and confident and cajoling like Mum's. But she won't be fooled.

'NO! Go away! It's cold and wet! No!' she pants, as the cool flannel touches her hot, pink skin. Undeterred, Dad keeps on. Up one arm, then the other arm. I go to the bathroom and get another facecloth. He manages to sit her up a bit. She's burning up.

Lucy has found the book, and brings a long cool drink upstairs for Grace. Dad hoists her up more in the bed.

'Come on, darling, take a drink for Daddy.'

'Is it medicine?' she asks suspiciously.

'NO!' we all reassure her.

Bit by bit, she sips the long glass of blackcurrant drink, forgetting that Dad is still sponging her down. Her eyes look drowsy and heavy, and she gives a huge shuddery, shaky kind of yawn.

'Off to bed, you two! You have school in the morning. I'll stay with her,' whispers Dad.

Lucy and I could drop, we're both so exhausted.

That selfish sod Conor is fast asleep, tossing and turning and mumbling to himself, like he always does. I am so tired, I feel I'll never get to sleep tonight at all.

Dad's voice is gentle outside in the girls' bedroom. He's singing Grace a song. It's funny, he's not the singing type usually, yet now in the stillness of the night his rough and out-of-tune voice is comforting.

'You are my sunshine, my only sunshine,
You make me happy when skies are grey ...'

I know that song so well. Hundreds of times when I was tiny it was sung to me. He used to sing to me often then. It's been so long since he did that. Sinking down into the pillows, I pull my stripy quilt up to my chin and join in those oh-so-familiar words:

'You'll never know, Greg, how much I love you,
Please don't take my sunshine away.'

Spots!

LUCY – *Wednesday*

Our kitchen looks like a bomb hit it. The tiles are so dirty that my shoes keep sticking to them. Maybe if I don't get too much homework tonight, I might give the floor a wash.

Dad looks like a zombie. His hair is dirty and standing on end. He has lost the belt of his dressing-gown and it keeps opening; even his pyjamas are all crumpled. He's moving slowly and stiffly this morning.

'My back is killing me,' he groans.

No wonder! Poor Dad. He slept the rest of last night on the edge of Grace's bed. He woke me up with all his snoring. Luckily, Grace is still asleep.

'Greg, what are you doing today?' Dad begins, as he helps himself to some cereal. Greg is annoyed with him. He's in his uniform and ready to leave for school.

'Sorry! But I can't help you, Dad. We've a real important chemistry practical today – and I'm busy for the *rest of the week*.' Greg pulls on his jacket, fixes his dark, straight hair and scoots out the back door, leaving Dad fuming.

I feel sorry for Dad. He's had a tough night. He's really done his best. Some fathers rant and rave and scream and swear when they're angry or in a temper. But Dad does none of those things. A hard, pulsing silence fills our kitchen. Conor is munching on a slice of cold toast, ignoring everything as usual.

'Dad! Grace won't be able to go to school today –' I begin.

'Thank you, Nurse Lucy, for your very obvious diagnosis of the problem,' he barks.

'Maybe Gran could come over ...' I suggest, but before I can say any more we notice the flushed, tousled figure standing in the doorway.

Grace is still half-asleep. Her tattered white rabbit dangles from one hand, and with the other she pulls up her pyjama-top. 'Daddy! Look at my spots!'

Dad and Conor and I stare at her. Vivid reddish-pink blotchy spots cover her stomach and neck and shoulders. There are more on her face, and I can see from her bare feet that the rash goes all the way down to her toes.

'I'm all spotty and scratchy!' she wails, her voice all wobbly, 'and I feel sick.'

The book on childhood illnesses is still upstairs from last night and I run up to our room to get it. I flick through, looking for something about rashes and spots.

Dad is busy on the phone when I get down again. 'Look, Gordon, I have a bit of a problem. No, it's not that I'll be delayed or late ...'

I point to the colour pictures in the medical book. Dad is trying to read and talk at the same time. His eyes widen. 'Listen, Gordon, I'm sorry, but the likelihood is that I'm going to have to take some time off ...'

Conor and I will be dead late for school, and get into more trouble. 'Dad, we've got to go,' I mouth to him and shove Conor towards the door. Grace's lip is starting to wobble, a sure sign that any minute now she'll start to cry again. I grab my schoolbag and the two of us manage to escape. Dad is going to have to survive on his own.

*   *   *

These days when you get in from school you never know exactly who's going to be there. So coming in and finding Dad at home is such a relief.

'Go easy, Lucy! Go easy! Quiet!' he whispers

anxiously. 'It's taken me an hour to get her to sleep.'

'I'll do my homework, Dad,' I say, 'and get the dinner then.'

'No, Luce. You're doing too much. You look tired. Anyway, it's about time I had a go at cooking something. You never know, I might be good at it! They say men make the best cooks!' he jokes.

Grace, looking like a baby, lies stretched out on the couch, fast asleep.

'The doctor was here,' he tells me.

'And?'

'Chickenpox and an ear infection, so no school for nearly ten days. Gran won't be able to come over in case she gets shingles, and Deirdre says she won't be able to mind Grace in case her own baby catches it too. So the only thing I could do was take some time off work.'

'I'm glad, Dad!'

'Glad?' he looks questioningly at me.

'What I mean is it'll be nice to have someone, I mean *you*, at home when we get in. The house won't seem so empty.'

Dad couldn't begin to understand what the last week has been like. I miss coming in and having

Mum to talk to. When Gran is here it's okay, but one day we went to Deirdre's and just watched TV until it was time to go home. It was boring. It'll be different with Dad, but ...

'Lucy! Are you listening to me? How does your Mum make that chicken pie we all like?' he asks.

'I'm not sure. It's probably in her special recipe book,' I say, 'the one where she writes down recipes from the radio and TV and magazines.' I find it stuffed between the paperbacks and Grace's books.

Dad sits down to read my mother's big writing, as if this is some kind of magic book – and once he learns the spells the magic will work!

Still, it's kind of nice ...

Rotas

CONOR – Friday

I have chickenpox too. Miss Boland saw the spots and phoned home, and Dad had to come to school and collect me. He's real annoyed, because now he has to take even more time off work to stay home and mind me.

Today we all got a postcard each from London. Mine is of the statue of Peter Pan in some park. Mum said it reminded her of me, and all the nights we read stories of pirates and ships and Never Never Land. I put the postcard on my pinboard beside my bed.

Dad is gone crazy. 'Our house is the most disorganised place I've ever been in! No systems. No routine!' he rants and raves.

It's not like this when Mum's here.

I heard him banging away on the computer, making out lists and work rotas. Maybe we'll have to get a housekeeper and go to a minder's every day.

Today the list went up. Dad stuck it on the kitchen door. Not too high, and not too low – so that everyone can read it. Practically the only thing Grace can read is her name: Grace. Now Dad is trying to teach her to read the words: TIDY AND PUT AWAY ALL TOYS NEATLY. She is getting the 'toys' bit, but she won't say the rest of the words. The whole month is worked out week by week.

'I'm not doing that job!' Greg insists when he gets home. 'Clean the toilets! No way!'

'There'll be no alteration to the schedule,' Dad informs us. 'The jobs have been allotted fairly and squarely, based on everyone's age, size and experience.' There it is in black and white:

1 DISINFECT, WASH AND CLEAN TOILETS: GREG.

Good man, Dad!

'I'm *not* doing it!'

'Greg, that's one of your jobs for the month of April and you will do it. Grace has to make sure to replace the toilet rolls, that should be okay for her.'

'It's not fair. Why am I landed with every rotten job in this stinking house? 1. Clean toilets. 2. Do the dustbins. What other smelly, disgusting jobs can you think of for me?' Greg shouts.

I feel like laughing. My jobs aren't too bad: clean the basins in the upstairs and downstairs bathrooms; empty the rubbish from upstairs every day; polish the mirrors; pack the dishwasher; sort out and match all the socks for the family.

Greg slams the kitchen door and goes off up to his room. The music blares so loud that Dad shouts at him. The angrier Greg gets the higher the volume, and the louder Dad has to shout. Maybe there is some justice after all.

* * *

A million socks – that's what this family must have. This job takes absolutely ages. One sock looks the exact same as another. The only ones that stand out are Grace's, as they're smaller and are mostly pink or have cute pictures of dogs and kittens and balloons on them. No wonder it takes her so long to make up her mind every day what ones she wants to wear.

Dad or Lucy must have done something wrong when they were doing the washing as all the socks seems to have come out the same size. What I need is some kind of sock measure. If I was an inventor that's the kind of useful thing I'd invent.

John called on his way home from school. Miss Boland gave him some schoolwork to leave in for me, so I won't fall further behind. He's had chicken-pox already so Dad allowed him in for a while.

He lives about two roads away, in a big redbrick house with a massive garden, acres of it. Right down at the back there's an old shed. It used to be a hen-house. He's going to start a club there. I'm not sure what kind of club it'll be but he told me to call when I'm let out again. I might join the club.

The Queen's House

GRACE – Monday

Mummy sent me a picture of the Queen of England's big house. I think she might have gone to visit her.

Today I did a big painting of me, so that Mum will remember what I look like. The little splodges are my spots, they're nearly gone now.

I did another painting of Conor. I made his spots big and red and blistery. Conor says that I am a BRAT.

Daddy will not let me send that picture of Conor to Mummy. He says it's unfair to do a picture of someone when they're not at their best, and Mummy might only get worried.

Growing Up

LUCY – Tuesday

Greg is so mean and such a pain! He said I was getting fat. He just loves to insult me. I hate my school uniform, and it's not my fault my blouse is so tight. I think I put it in too hot a wash and it must have shrunk, or else I'm getting bigger! Brenda says she jiggles and that I'm starting too. It's so embarrassing.

I wish Mum was here. Brenda's mum is getting her a bra on Saturday. If Mum doesn't come back soon, I'm going to end up the only one in my class without a bra or proper body-top.

There is no way that I'm going into a shop on my own for one. And I just couldn't face telling Dad. Oh please, God! Let Mum come home soon.

Cutbacks

GREG – *Thursday*

'Come in here, boys! I want to talk to both of you,' Dad summons Conor and me into the living room. Conor shuffles in ahead of me. 'Sit down!' he tells us. It must be bad if he wants us to sit down.

'This separation business with your Mum –'

'Her leaving you,' I interrupt.

'This separation,' he continues, 'naturally, it's having an effect on each of us. We all miss her, and ... well, home is just not the same. We'll just have to try to pull together a bit better. Now, Lucy is doing more than her fair share. The two of you have just got to pull your weight more.'

'But I minded Grace the other day! I brought her out with me.'

Dad listens to my protest. 'But you do nothing to help with cooking, and that's a huge responsibility. And I noticed *you* left a trail of biscuit crumbs all over the carpet yesterday, Conor, just after Lucy had finished hoovering it.'

Conor still says nothing.

'And did you hoover it up?' demands Dad.

Conor just shrugs his shoulders.

'You are both taking advantage of Lucy and her kind nature. It will just have to stop. Is that clear?' Dad states firmly.

'Loud and clear!' we both agree.

Conor disappears as soon as he can. Dad settles down to read the newspaper.

'Dad?' I ask.

He looks up.

'Dad! I was wondering if you could give me a bit of extra money?'

'*More* pocket money?'

'No! Well, I suppose ... sort of.'

'What did you do with last week's money?'

'It's gone!'

'Just like that! Greg, money doesn't grow on trees.'

'A few of us went bowling, and on Saturday I went to the cinema. And ... now I really need a new tennis racquet.'

'But you have one already!'

'Yeah, but it's ancient, and it hasn't got the power I need. I need a graphite racquet.'

'How much do they cost?'

He pales when I tell him. 'It's out of the question, Greg!'

'Look, Dad! I really need it. You know I'm good at tennis, and with a racquet like that I'd be certain to qualify and do well in the school championships.'

'Greg! I'm not made of money. And things are very tight at the moment.'

'But Dad, you've a good job, you make good money,' I remind him.

'Greg, you're old enough to understand that since your Mum left my earnings have dropped. I'm losing most of my overtime and a lot of my travel and mileage expenses. And I'm very unlikely to get my half-yearly sales bonus like I normally do. I'll be lucky if I even make my target sales at the rate things are going!' He runs his fingers through his hair which is just starting to show a tinge of grey. 'To be honest, Greg, I'm really worried!' Fine lines are etched round his eyes and he looks kind of tired. 'We seem to be spending a huge amount of money – even the grocery bills have shot up. Deirdre is very good, giving a hand minding Grace and the others after school some days, but at this stage I have to pay her something. We can't keep on relying on other people's generosity!'

This hadn't occurred to me. Dad and Mum used to fight a lot about money, and Mum wanted to try to make a bit of extra money herself.

'Then ... about the tennis racquet ...' I venture.

'No, Greg! It's not possible. We're all going to have to cut back, including you! Three nights this week, you know, you left the immersion on. Our electricity bill will be enormous, and heaven knows what the phone bill will be like with all these extra calls to London! Look, I'm going out for a walk.'

Off he goes leaving me to stew over it.

Later on, Lucy comes in to watch the television and I tell her, expecting her to be on my side.

'Dad's right about cutting back,' she says firmly.

'But, Luce! You know I need that racquet!'

'Well, maybe you should try and get a part-time job or something,' she says, 'then you could save up for it yourself.'

A part-time job! Maybe Lucy is right, maybe that's the answer.

The Picnic

LUCY – *Saturday*

At last Grace and Conor are better again. Dad has been at home all week looking after them and cooking. There were a few disasters, like the day he burnt the lamb chops and the kitchen filled with heavy, black smoke. He's a bit more relaxed too, and he sits down with me when I come home from school every day. He asks me all about my friends and school and everything.

Summer is coming at last. All the bulbs Mum put down in the garden are blooming. The gnarled old cherry tree outside our driveway is just starting to show a hint of blossom. It's a bit cold, but we're going on a picnic – our first picnic of the year!

Dad went down to the local delicatessen and bought French bread, a tub of coleslaw and a tub of potato salad, and loads of other things. So we have a choice of fillings. I'm having tuna and lettuce. Grace is having salami. Conor is spreading thick dollops of chocolate spread on his – gross! I made a load of chocolate Rice Krispie buns, and Dad has bought iced buns and biscuits and two bags of jelly-babies. Last night Dad went up to the attic and brought down the big red ice-box that we use for picnics and outings.

'Everyone is better now,' he announced. 'We're going to have some fun.'

He's putting the plastic plates and cups in a box. 'We're still a family, you know! We can still have a good time!' he says.

It's funny, but today, with his denim shirt and jeans on, Dad looks kind of young and sort of like Greg, except for the wrinkles on his forehead and the bits of grey in his hair. I think he's very lonely. Sometimes one of Mum's friends phones to see how he's doing, or one of the men from his company meets him for lunch, or after work. But late at night, when we go to bed, he has no one to talk to.

'Where are we going? Where? Where?' Grace keeps pestering him, all excited.

'It's a surprise, pet,' he tells her.

'But I must know,' she begs.

'Why?'

"Cos ..."

'*Bec*ause,' he corrects her.

''Cos – I've got to know whether to bring my wellington boots or my bucket and spade.'

'Oh! I see,' Dad laughs.

'Picnics are always to the seaside or the country,' she replies, in a know-it-all voice.

'Just wait and see,' says Dad.

*   *   *

The car climbs the winding roads through the leafy spring countryside, up into the Dublin mountains. Then we go higher up on foot, up steep forest mountain paths. We're all panting. Still, I love the smell of pine-needles, and the soft crunch of them under your feet as you walk, and the dull thump as you push your way through the moss and ferns.

Greg has to pull Grace along. Conor looks kind of pale. He's a bit too skinny for a ten-year-old. His cut-off jeans flap around his bony white legs, and he's wearing old runners of Greg's. He should have put on socks with them – he'll end up with blisters.

'Come on! Keep going!' Dad yells at us.

He leads the way and we follow him like a scout troop. No matter what way you look, all you can see is trees and more trees. The further we march, the further away home seems to be – I mean what has happened, Mum and all that. Suddenly I can spot snatches of blue and glimmers of yellow-gold, one patch, then another, as sunlight dazzles through the trees at the end of the path.

'Top of the world!' shouts Grace.

And do you know, she's right. Once we come out of the trees into the clearing, we realise that we are near the top of the mountain. The countryside and fields fall away below us. When I look downwards the land seems to tilt and almost makes me dizzy. Dublin is spread out in the distance – factories, offices and high church steeples, all like a little toy town. The river Liffey meanders like a shiny, blue-grey snail trail, through the places we know and love, down to the docks, then out into the vast blue brightness of Dublin Bay. Conor says he can see our road, and Grace says she can see our house! The roof of our house is the same as about a million others, so how the hell can they tell? A noonday haze wobbles over the city.

'Lucy! Grab hold of Grace. I'd forgotten how dangerous this place can be!' Dad interrupts me.

Dad spreads out a blue-and-white check tablecloth

over an area of flat rock and patchy grass. Opening the cool-box he takes out the food and drink. Greg and Conor are like two savages and pull at the cold meats. They're always starving! Food is their main worry. Grace decides to try a bit of my tuna sandwich roll. 'Ugh!' she shouts, then she spits it out.

Dad stretches himself out in the sun and puts on his sunglasses. He sips from a can of orange.

'Isn't this place just perfect!' he announces.

'Yeah,' we all agree, munching our food.

'Go on! Breathe in deeply,' he's getting a bit carried away now, 'fill your lungs with that pure fresh air. You know, my father used to bring me up here when I was a boy. The beauty of it always takes my breath away. Your mother and I used to drive up here the odd Sunday in our courting days, then when we married we used to bring you two, Greg and Lucy, dragging carrycots and nappies and sunshades and bottles with us.

'Up here, it's hard to think of ordinary, mundane things. You just have to relax. You know, in all the years it has hardly changed. The city has spread out more below, but way up here it's still the same – even without your mother it's still beautiful!'

Greg looks embarrassed, but I want Dad to tell us more now. Instead, he props himself against a rock and concentrates on eating his salad. Grace has discovered a few insects, and is trying to pen them in with a ring of stones, but they keep climbing over and escaping on her.

The boys want to back-track and explore a bit. Dad's a bit edgy about it. 'Greg, you're to take care of Conor,' he warns. 'It's easy to trip or fall up here, so no messing or stunts, okay?'

I decide to stay and mind Grace while Dad relaxes. Monday morning he'll be back to work fulltime and he still hasn't sorted out what to do about us! I wonder why he and Mum stopped coming up here. Maybe they got too busy or forgot how nice it is?

One hour slips into another, the boys return finally, the late afternoon sun gets weaker, and here on the mountain it's getting cooler. The food is gone and I'm starving again.

'Dad, I'm hungry,' whines Conor. Dad ignores him. Grace is getting bored too and is looking for attention. 'Dad! Can we go home now?' pleads Conor.

I can tell that Dad doesn't want to go home – he just wants to stay here and forget everything.

'It will get dark, and we'll be lost in the forest like Hansel and Gretel,' warns Grace.

'Don't be silly, Gracey! We'll be going home real soon,' I assure her.

'There's no trail and nobody will find us ...' She's really getting scared now.

'Dad, come on!' Greg stands over Dad, demanding attention. 'Come on, Dad! Let's get moving!' His voice is serious. 'Here, let me give you a hand. It's getting cold and we don't want to be stuck up here in the dark.'

Greg's hands are big and strong-looking, and he chews his nails. Dad's are paler and thinner and kind of freckled. Dad just stares up at him.

'Dad, everything is packed, and Grace is pretty whacked,' I add, standing with Greg in front of him.

'All right, all right,' he grumbles and lets himself be pulled up. 'Let's get this show on the road, then. I'll lead the way.'

Now with the sun gone down, we all pull on our sweatshirts. My skin is warm but inside I feel a strange kind of chill.

'He's not going to leave us here,' Grace whispers to me behind Dad's back. She begins to run, trying to keep up with him.

It's all downhill on the way back and should be a lot easier. But in the dusk we keep losing our footing and stumbling over twisted roots and rocks. Every time I try to go a bit faster I feel out of control, as the descent is so steep. Conor slides in the dirt beside me. He grazes the backs of his legs and hands when he tries to stop himself falling.

'Dad, wait!' he calls frantically.

But Dad just keeps on going. Conor brushes the dirt off himself, and ignores the pain. Greg takes Grace by the hand to steady her so she won't fall too. We slip and slide and skid the whole way down the mountain track until we get to the safety of our car.

'Will we stop for chips?' Dad enquires as he starts up the engine. Nobody answers. The car beams flood the silent roadway with light, and a scared wood-pigeon breaks through the pines as we head for home.

The Club

CONOR – *Monday*

Gran is on the phone when I get in from school. I don't mean to listen, but I know she's really annoyed.

It must be Mum she's talking to. 'Well, Vanessa!' I hear her say, 'things are sort of all right here. But it's been three weeks now, you know! Naturally, there have been upsets,' she lowers her voice, and stares at me, 'but Christopher is handling the situation as best he can.'

I get a glass of water from the tap.

'Yes! Thank you. I am doing my best, but I'm afraid I had plans ...' Her voice is getting more edgy and sharp. I sip the water and hope she'll forget about me. 'No! No, Vanessa, Grace has gone across the road to play, only Conor is here beside me.'

I try to get past her, but Gran shoves the phone into my hand.

'Conor, pet! Is that you?' the voice is kind, caring and the same.

'Yes, Mum!'

'How are you, Conor? How is school going?'

School! Why does it always come down to school?

'Fine,' I lie. No point in telling her I only got six out of twenty right in my last spelling test and that I'm two chapters behind in my reading book and in my workbook.

'Where are you, Mum?'

'I'm still in London, Conor. I've started a computer course. Your Aunt Mary is being very good to me, letting me stay and all that. This is a huge city – millions of people rushing around the place. I'm almost afraid to put a foot in the Underground during rush hour. You know, you could get lost in a place like this. But there are hundreds of museums and galleries and places to visit. Some day, I'll bring you over here so you can see for yourself.'

'That's nice!' I try to sound interested. 'Is it sunny?'

'Actually it rained all this morning. At the moment it's grey and drizzly, even a bit misty – I suppose a bit like home.' I can hear the choke in her voice. She's homesick. Good!

'Mum! How long are you going to stay there? How

long is this separation thing going to last? When are you coming home?'

She gives a little cough. 'I'm not sure yet, pet!' Then she changes the subject. 'Are you helping your Dad and your Gran?'

'Yep!'

'Are you all eating okay?'

'Yep!'

'Are you sleeping okay?'

'Yep!'

'Conor, don't say "yep". Say "yes, Mum"! As if you *mean* it, Conor!' she pleads.

'Yes, Mum! I really miss you.'

She takes in a big breath. 'I miss you too, Conor, you know.' It sounds a bit like she's crying. Triumph tickles the tips of my fingers. I wrap the phone cord around my thumb. She is hurting too. I can tell. It's in her voice.

'Conor! Will you tell the others I phoned? I don't want you to worry about any of this. It will get sorted out! I promise! I'll be in touch again soon. Bye, bye, love!'

'Goodbye, Mum!'

*   *   *

I've got to get out of the house and away from Gran. She wants me to repeat word-for-word everything Mum said. I tell her I'm not a tape-recorder.

'It's important,' she says.

The minute she turns her back I escape.

It takes exactly six minutes to get to John's house. His road is long and winding, and all the houses have driveways that are cobbled. Each house has a name on its gate or pillar instead of just a number. His is called 'Byways'. The paint on the gate is bright and shiny white and his lawn is as green and as neat as can be. His Dad is a surgeon, so a man comes to do the garden. His Dad is always busy, and has no time for gardening or ordinary things. Sometimes he even forgets about John. His Mum opens the door.

'Round the back, Conor! That's where they've gone!' She points to the side passageway.

I go as quietly as I can. Down beyond the giant lilac tree, I can see the shed. The windows are all steamed up. I tiptoe towards it. There's talk going on inside. That means the club is on. I cough and make noise – better to give them some warning in case they're talking about me. I half-push and half-knock on the wooden door.

When I go inside they all ignore me. John just sort

of nods and points to an old box near him. I lower myself down on it and hope there are no nails sticking up out of it.

John is busy writing: THE RULES OF OUR CLUB on a large piece of white paper. 'Code names?' he asks and sucks on the lid of his pen.

'We have to think of a special name for all seven of us,' Alan explains. He's a year older than the rest of us and goes to a different school, but he lives across the road. His face is long and thin and he is a right know-it-all. His Dad is a professor in the university.

'Brains!' says Ian. 'That can be your name.'

Alan considers for a second, then nods. He likes the name. It suits him.

Brian is sitting on the edge of the box with me, his long, lanky legs and big, overgrown feet sprawled out in front of him. I can tell he's thinking about what awful name they'll give him. Theo stares at him, looking at every fault. Brian is fidgeting and nervous.

'What about "The Rocket" for Brian?' suggests Alan.

A shudder of relief goes through the slats of the

wooden box and Brian shoots up, nearly sending me flying.

'Yeah! That's great – I'm The Rocket,' Brian shouts, delighted with himself.

Soon it will be my turn. I'm not the tallest or the smallest, I'm not fat, and I'm not the skinniest. My hair is mousey and ordinary. There's nothing special about me!

Everyone else is staring at Mark. He's a big kid and usually sits at the back of the class. In school they call him Fatso or Big Boy. He's always last to do everything and never seems to rush himself. Ian is looking at him, thinking of names, and, I guess, working out which name will be the worst. He is going to say ...

'The Giant.' I can't believe I said it. 'Mark should be The Giant.'

Brian and Alan agree with me and I can see John is thinking about it. Mark just sits there and nods his big, smiling face.

'Giant,' he repeats. 'Yep! That's me!'

John writes it down on the list. 'What about my own name?' he asks. 'I think ... because I own the clubhouse ...'

'You're not the leader,' insists Ian.

'But it *is* my house and my garden.'

Ian looks up from under his eyelids, narrowing his eyes.

'What about Keymaster?' volunteers John.

We all look at Ian, trying to decipher his reaction. He takes ages and ages considering and making John squirm, then, finally, he agrees, and suddenly turns around and points at Ciaran. 'Well, he'll be Speccy or Blind Bat!'

Ciaran's skin is getting pinker and redder, and his thick glasses have become steamed up. He takes them off and rubs them on a hanky, staring at them intently. Blinking, he whispers 'Batman' half hopefully.

'Blind Bat,' Ian and John announce in unison, smirking at each other.

They keep passing over me. What will I do if they call me 'Nobody'? I reckon it's better to think of something myself before they land a name on me. I rattle my brains trying to think of something. Time is running out.

'I'll be The Dolphin,' I say. They all just stare at me, already bored. I know it's not very original. I grab a spare piece of paper and draw a strange-looking fish – a dolphin. 'That's my signature,' I state.

Ian simply shrugs his shoulders and John says, 'The Dolphin. Not bad.' They lift up my drawing and stare at it. 'Good idea!'

A few seconds later everyone in the club is drawing their own symbol – to be used and known only by us club members!

Hard Knock

GREG – *Wednesday*

We're almost an hour waiting in casualty. Lots of old people and mothers with children are in the queue ahead of us. I hate hospitals, even the smell of them is enough to make me feel like throwing up. It must be the stuff they use to wash the floors and walls with. Such bad luck! Why did I bother trying to tackle Barry like that? I know why – last match of the season and I was trying to show how good I was. He was ready for me, and even though he's smaller, he's much stronger. That damn disinfectant stuff! In a second I'm going to be sick. My eyes feel as if someone has squirted something sticky in them, and it's a hell of a job to keep them open, and my head, it's so heavy I don't think my neck will hold it up much longer.

Coach is like a crazy man, walking up and down looking for attention. I just want to curl up on the waiting bench and sleep. Strange arms are half-pulling me and forcing me to wake and get on my feet. All the pensioners turn their sad eyes to me as I try to concentrate on standing and letting Coach and the nurse lead me to one of the funny little cubicles.

My stomach gives an almighty heave, and the nurse gets the white plastic bowl there just in the nick of time. Coach jumps out of the way, then he pulls back the curtain and is shouting and looking for a doctor. The bed in casualty is so narrow that I am in danger of falling out of it. I have to try and remember where I am.

A doctor has come over, and Coach is shouting at her now. The doctor tells him if he doesn't quieten down he will have to wait outside. My head is muzzy and my mouth is dry.

'Nurse! Nurse, may I have a drink of water, please?' I beg.

She ignores me and disappears out through the yellow-and-white striped curtains.

'Greg! You'll be fine,' Coach tries to reassure me.

The doctor pushes by him, and shoves a little torch thing in my eyes. My head is throbbing and spinning.

'It was only a bad knock, a rugby tackle,' Coach rambles on. I can tell by the way the doctor reacts that she is not a rugby fan. 'Should I phone the boy's mother?' Coach asks.

The doctor nods. I want to tell him.

'I'll be back in a minute, Greg, I'm just going to use the phone.'

Coach Hudson exits from the cubicle before I get a chance to say a word.

I close my eyes. The doctor and two nurses are talking. I feel too tired to listen. I just hear a low mumble and see faint blurs of white.

A nurse wipes my face and eyebrow. It stings.

'Greg, you need a few stitches.' The doctor's voice is distant.

They can do what they want with me, I don't care! Suddenly I feel so cold and the nurse puts a warm blanket on me.

*   *   *

It is almost dark when I wake up. At first I can't remember where I am. White walls and that smell.

Coach is sitting by my bed. He's reading the evening newspaper – wouldn't you know it, the sports section.

'Coach?'

He shoots up with fright. 'Ah! You're awake, Greg, that's good!'

'Where am I?'

'You're in Saint Gabriel's, the hospital. They're keeping you in for observation; it's standard procedure. You got a bad knock on the head.' He pats me on the hand. 'How're you feeling?'

'Sore!'

'Only to be expected.'

'Sore all over.' Even as I say it, I realise how true it is. I put my hand up to my face and head. Then I notice two of my fingers are in a splint and my face is all swollen.

'Take it easy, Greg! You have a few stitches.'

A grey-faced old man in the next bed starts a racking cough. Coach looks uncomfortable, and turns his chair the other way. 'Old and sick – comes to us all,' he mutters under his breath.

From outside in the corridor, I hear heavy, familiar

footsteps, and a voice asking directions. Dad!

'Greg!' He's suddenly standing at the bed. He bends down and hugs me close, smelling of sweat and garlic salami and home.

'I got here as quick as I could.' Dad looks me up and down and only then seems to notice Coach.

'Mr Hudson, isn't it?'

'Nice to meet you again, Mr Dolphin. We met briefly last term at the Matthews match.'

'Christopher, please.'

'I brought the boy here straight away, and I've stayed with him since. He's coming round.'

'I appreciate it, Mr Hudson.'

'I tried to phone your home and get in touch with your wife, and so did the school secretary,' Coach says. 'But, no luck.'

'I know, I'm sorry.' Dad doesn't bother to offer an explanation.

'Greg will be okay. It's all part of rugby. They all get knocks but generally they bounce back,' Mr Hudson says, then adds, 'Look, I'd better leave the two of you, I have to get home.'

Dad nods, and Mr Hudson after a few minutes says goodbye, then finally disappears, his bulky figure ambling out the door of the ward.

My Dad sits in silence, staring at me, then hugs me again. 'Thank God you're all right, Greg! You can't imagine what it's been like driving here.'

He holds me so close to him that I can hear his heartbeat. When I was small, I used to sit on his lap and we would watch the sport on the television. He'd turn the sound down low and I would listen to the bump, bump, bump of his heartbeat. He moves, embarrassed, and releases me.

'Gran is at home now, minding the others.'

I don't actually care about the rest of them or home ... at the moment I feel it is just Dad and me, back in those long-ago days and I want to hear that bump, bump, bump again.

'Look, Greg! Is that your doctor?'

I nod my sore, heavy head.

'I want to talk to her. I'll be back in a minute.'

Doctor Scully is talking to a large middle-aged man who is wearing a big blue-green bow tie. He must be another doctor. Spotting my Dad, they both turn to talk to him.

Dad is all anxious and excited. I can tell, by the way he's standing and rubbing the back of his neck.

Red Riding Hood

LUCY – Saturday

The swimming pool is packed. The screaming and shouting and splashing bounces off the walls and echoes all around and the sun beats down on us through the monstrous, domed, glassy roof. It's like being in a giant steambath. Greg has stayed at home in bed playing his walkman because he's not well enough to go swimming yet.

Dad is half-walking and half-swimming as Grace bobs along in her armbands beside him. I want to practise lengths, to get a good steady rhythm going. The chlorine is very strong today and it stings my eyes. Everyone will think I've been crying.

Conor is standing at the side of the pool, peering into the water and trying to make up his mind whether to dive or not.

'Lucy!' Dad calls. 'Will you stay with Grace for a few minutes? I want to go for a bit of a swim on my own.'

Grace pretends to be a mermaid and splashes

along beside me. Dad swims strongly through the crowds of learners and proud parents and weekend swimmers.

Every weekend now it's the same. Dad takes us somewhere special: the zoo, the wax museum, the National Gallery. You name it, we've been there. At this stage we're bumping into the same people, mostly dads and their kids. You can spot them a mile off as the dads are usually trying to read the paper and have a bit of peace. Our Dad doesn't like us hanging around the house. 'We all need to broaden our minds.' That's what he keeps telling us. We might even be going away with him for a few days.

Gran says that Dad is a reformed character. I'm not sure what that means, but I guess it means a whole lot better than he was. Last week he went to our school and told the principal about Mum and the trial separation. I wish he hadn't, because now Mrs O'Malley is always watching me. Every morning she asks me, 'How are things at home?' If I yawn or look tired, she wants to know if I'm getting enough sleep. At lunch-break she walks down by my table and secretly checks that I have enough food and that it is nutritious!

'Come on, you lot! Out of the pool!' Dad shouts.

'The whistle is due to go in about four minutes.'

Grace's teeth are chattering. A quick splash under the warm shower, and then I wrap her in her big yellow towel. I'm freezing too and I hate the feel of cold, wet togs sticking to my skin, but if I don't do her first she'll get all upset.

'Grace! Sit on the bench! Sit still!'

The floor of the dressing room is really wet, and if your clothes fall on the ground it's just awful. Grace keeps hopping around the place. She knocks her T-shirt down, and I put it on backwards, hoping she won't notice the wet patch near the shoulders. Then I drag on my own clothes and quick as a wink head out to the car and the others.

Dad and Conor are busy not talking, listening to the radio. With his wet hair and nervous face, Conor looks a bit like a twitchy mouse.

'Well! Where is it to be?' asks Dad, yawning.

'The shopping centre,' pleads Conor.

'The park and the swings,' begs Grace.

Since Dad hates shopping it's a good guess where we'll end up. I don't want to go with them. I say I want to be dropped at Gran's.

*   *   *

It seems strange to be standing here outside my grandmother's front door. I feel like Little Red Riding Hood come to visit, except that I'm wearing a red sweatshirt instead of the cloak. Dad has gone to the playground with the others. I press the bell, and hear the chimes ring through the narrow hall. No reply! Maybe she had to go out. I should have told them to wait. I ring it again and listen for the jangle.

I could let myself in. Granny keeps a key hidden under the pot of geraniums on the left-hand side of the door, just in case of emergencies. Dad keeps telling her that it is too dangerous, that a burglar might find it some day and break into her house. But Gran is always losing and forgetting things – her bag, her cardigan, her glasses, the book she's reading – so I can understand it. This is her way of making sure she can always get back into her own house. I wait a minute or two, listening to the sound of magpies fighting in the overhead trees. Just as I crouch down to lift the flowerpot, the front door opens.

'Lucy!' Surprise and accusation fill her voice.

'Hi, Gran!' I blush.

'I've changed my hiding place,' she confides. 'It's under the rock near that lavender bush now.' I nod.

'Don't bother telling your father about it!' she laughs.

She leads me through the dim, narrow hallway to her cluttered breakfast-room. The French doors are open, and I've obviously interrupted her in the middle of doing the garden.

'Is everything all right, Lucy?' Her face is anxious.

All I can manage is a nod. It doesn't fool her for a single moment.

'Are you sure, Lucy?'

'I felt like calling ... to see you ...' I stutter.

'That's very nice,' she says softly. 'I'm a lucky woman to have such a good, considerate grand-daughter. Come on in and sit down! I was just due to make myself a cup of tea anyway. Then you can come and give me a hand with a bit of weeding.'

She fills the kettle and lights her old gas cooker. Her kitchen is small and neat and smells slightly of pine disinfectant. 'It's nice to have a bit of company. Weekends, I'm usually on my own.'

She takes down two white china teacups, two saucers and pale pink flower-patterned plates. At home all we ever use is mugs. Two chocolate biscuits and a big, knobbly, nutty one on each plate. Then she sits on her chair watching me while we wait for the water to boil. I pull my knees up under me. I'm sitting on the cat's chair. His two cushions are covered in fluff and give off the smell of cat.

'Any news from your mother in the last few days?' she asks, taking a bite of biscuit.

'She phones. She phones quite a lot, actually,' I tell her. 'You know, sometimes you'd think Mum and Dad were best friends. I think my Mum is lonely. She misses us!'

'I'm sure she does,' mutters Gran. 'Act in haste, repent at leisure!'

Steam blows up from the kettle and sprays the tiles with a damp mist. Gran bustles over, makes a pot of tea and carries it to the table.

'Being left behind – it's a hard thing,' she says. 'When I was a little girl, Lucy, not much older than you, a terrible thing happened. One day my father walked out the door. He just opened that farmhouse door in West Cork, where we grew up – he knew every stick and inch of the place – he pushed open that door as if he was going across the yard to feed the hens or check the pigs or do something in the barn. Only this morning it was different. My grand-father sat in the corner of the kitchen, not saying a word, smoking his pipe. My mother made a breakfast so big that none of us could eat it. Usually she hated wasting food but this morning it was different. My father hugged me and told me to be a "good girl" and help my mother! He shook my brother Daniel by the hand and then he was gone, out across the muddy yard, a bag slung over his shoulder. Those were war times and he had joined up.'

She stops, and I can tell she's remembering every bit of it.

'Did he die?'

'As good as! His ship was torpedoed and he was left floating in the sea for a day. He was sent to a hospital in England, then back to the front. He came home about three years later. My grandfather had died by then, but it seemed to me that my father took over his position in our household. Most of the day, he just sat in the corner by the fire. A young man had left us, and an old, broken man came home.'

'But he didn't die!'

'No! Just inside! I can still remember what it was like.'

Her hand reaches out and touches mine. Her knuckles are knobbly and she must have hurt one of her fingers as the nail is black-looking. Her wedding ring seems loose and big on her thin finger. They are old hands. They make me want to cry. She sips her tea and nibbles her biscuit.

Then the tears come, dropping on to the plate and on her tablecloth.

She pulls a tissue from her sleeve and passes it to me silently.

I am crying for my Granny and her old working hands. I am crying for a man who left his farm and family, and never came back the same. I am crying for my Mum. I wish she hadn't had to go away. She must be so sad. And I guess if I'm honest I'm crying for ME. It's as if a big dam is bursting inside me. I can't stop all the sadness leaking out of me.

Gran just watches and says nothing. She passes me tissue after tissue and puts the used ones in the bin. After a while there are fewer tissues needed. Gran wets a towel and wipes my eyes and face as if she's cleaning a baby or a toddler.

'Feel better now, pet?'

It's funny, but I do – kind of empty and drained out.

Old Max comes in, jumps up on my lap, and makes

himself into a ball. He purrs gruffly as I pet him.

'Don't get too comfortable there, young lady! Remember all those weeds are a-growing.'

I feel kind of shaky and wobbly, and the sunlight blinds my eyes for a second when I step outside. Gran's garden is about three times the size of ours. Dad keeps on saying that it is too big for her to manage on her own, and that she should move to an apartment, but she really loves this house and garden. She knows every leaf and flower, and watches it all change from day to day, season to season. She and Max need this garden.

But in one corner there are a lot of weeds, trailing and sneaking and winding everywhere. I pull them or dig them up, making sure to get the roots.

At teatime, Gran makes us a tray of sandwiches, all tiny and neatly cut with no crusts. Chicken, tomato, salad with mayonnaise. Funny, the fresh air and work have left me starving. As I wolf down the sandwiches, I notice Gran has taken only one. Old people don't eat half as much as people my age.

'Growing bodies need good food,' Gran says, watching me eat.

Gran must be the nicest old person that I know.

She was very pretty – well, still is. Every week she goes to the hairdresser and has her hair washed and set. Once the hairdresser put in a bluey rinse by mistake, instead of the honey-gold that she likes, and she was so upset. My Mum had to drive over to calm her down and then ring the hairdresser and complain. She didn't want any of us to see her like that. She takes lots of vitamins because she is real scared of falling and breaking her hip.

On my way to the bathroom, I stop outside her spare bedroom. It is very small. A big black plastic sack full of scraps of material fills the floor. She's making a patchwork quilt. Bits of it are pinned together and hang over the velour chair and the bed. She has been working on it for about a year.

'Gran!'

She comes out into the corridor and catches me looking at the room. She knows what I'm thinking.

'Lucy! This room is such a mess. Some day soon I'll get round to fixing it up, and maybe then you and little Grace could come and sleep over.'

'Could I stay tonight?' I plead.

'No!' she shakes her head. 'It's not that I don't want you, Lucy, it's just that it wouldn't be a very good idea at the moment – your Dad needs you to be at home.'

'Oh!'

My grandmother picks up an old photo of Dad, taken when he was a little boy. A boy who looks a bit like Greg, but with longer, floppier hair, and dressed in a school uniform, stares out. He's trying to smile but there's something shy about him.

'That was taken in his last year in primary school. He was about eleven then. Worried about something. He was a good child but it was always hard to know what he was thinking about.'

I stare into the blue-grey eyes of my father as a child, trying to guess.

Gran is searching for something, rummaging in the pocket of her navy cardigan. 'Got them!' She dangles the car keys. 'Come on, Lucy, pet! Let's get you home!'

Runaway

CONOR – *Monday*

The club house seems small and crowded and stuffy today, as if there isn't space for everyone. I scan the corners for a spare seat.

'Get lost, Conor!' Ian mumbles at me.

'Get lost, yourself!' I try to sound tough. Ian is doing his best to block my way, so that I can't sit down. John is pretending to look at a book, so he doesn't have to see what's going on.

Brian is shoving up to make a space for me, but Alan gives him a kick with his mud-stained boots. I pretend I'm happy to stand, and fiddle in my anorak pocket for the remaining half of the chocolate bar Dad got me last night. I'll put it in the club food-box instead of eating it myself.

'Excuse me!' I brush past Ian, 'I want to put something in the tin.'

Ciaran passes me the old biscuit box. It has a pattern of snowmen and Christmas trees on the outside. It is half-full – a packet of mints, some chewing-gum, two bags of crisps and a few loose toffees.

'Hope that hasn't gone off!' warns Alan.

'No! I only got it last night, I saved most of it.' I shove it in with the rest of the stuff, making sure the paper is wrapped good and tight around it before I put the lid back on.

John coughs and begins, 'Now, about next weekend – we need to plan this hike we're going on.'

This sounds interesting.

'What day are we going?' I ask.

'*We* are going on Saturday,' mumbles John.

'Sounds good!' I can't help smiling.

'Yeah! Sound's great, Dolphin, 'cos you won't be there!' jeers Ian. I glare at him but say nothing.

John blushes. 'My Dad is dropping us off early in the morning on his way to play golf in Rock Mount, and we're going to hike the whole way back. It's a few miles.'

'Not for weaklings,' sneers Ian.

'The problem is, Conor, that my Dad can only take four in the car,' mutters John, holding his head down.

'I have piano lessons on Saturday mornings,' Ciaran nods, relieved, 'so I couldn't go anyway.'

Mark doesn't say a word, just stares at his bulging trainers. I guess he is used to this kind of thing. He should explode, grab them, fling them round the room. What the hell kind of Giant is he anyway?

'It stinks!' The words spurt out before I know it. 'It's not fair! There should have been a draw!'

'You unhappy with this club, Dolphin? Well, you know what you can do!' Ian threatens.

I hate them.

'Take a hike!' he jeers.

They all crack up laughing.

I grab the tin, fling off the lid, take back my chocolate and two extra toffees and ram them into my pocket. Somehow, the crisp bags burst and I scatter the crumbs like golden confetti all over the others and make a run out the door.

'Get back in here and tidy this!' roars Alan.

'Go stuff!' I yell and take off.

My sleeve is soggy and shiny and my eyes must be red and bulgy by the time I get to our house.

Lucy is busy doing her homework, with that big frown that gives her train-tracks across her forehead.

'Luce?'

'Uh!'

She's chewing her pencil and trying to work out a load of 'a+b+x+y's written on her page.

'You okay, Conor?' she asks without looking up.

'Sure!'

'Hey, Dad left a note for you on the fridge.'

A red plastic number 5 pins my father's words to me against the white door: 'CONOR. YOU PACKED THE DISHWASHER THE WRONG WAY THIS MORNING. PLEASE RE-DO IT. - DAD.

Sure is interesting. I get the message loud and clear. Nobody believes that I can do anything right. Now that Mum is gone, nobody really cares about me any more. This whole family stinks!

Suddenly I find myself bombing up the stairs, pulling my rucksack out of the wardrobe, and starting to fill it.

I've had enough of them all.

*   *   *

Walking, you go where you want, when you want ... that's my motto.

I'm a good walker. I often see other kids whingeing on walks, having to be bribed with sweets and ice-cream every step of the way. But once you get into a stride, it's a bit like running.

My heart is punching faster, urging me to start jogging, but I know if I do I'll get tired far faster and won't be able to go a long distance. So it's walk, walk, walk.

My post-office savings book and my money are in my jacket pocket. I try and jiggle the shoulder of my bag so that it isn't so heavy, but the tug and pressure is making my neck and back ache already.

At first I thought I might head for the city. Catch a bus right into the centre of town. But the streets are dark and lonely at night, and once the big shops are shut only a few restaurants and pubs and clubs are open, places kids aren't let into. From the park near our house, I can see the sea, all the ships and boats coming in and out of Dublin Bay. I like ships and the foamy pattern of white they weave through the spread of sea-blue. I want to see them up close, maybe even go on one. I sort of know the direction I'm heading, but it's a pity I didn't bring that compass I got to go with the water-bottle and belt and torch set about two Christmasses ago. It might still work.

It's too dangerous to thumb a lift, so I keep my head down and act as if I live around here and I'm on my way home from PE or something. Don't want to meet anyone who would know Mum or Dad in case they stop me.

The sprawling shopping centre is closing, a file of cars is pushing out of the car park and joining the traffic lanes. One by one the shop lights go out, like giant eyes closing down, leaving a glassy grey shape, still and dark. The security man nods to me as he pulls over the low metal barrier when the last car leaves. From here I know the road to take, and most of it is downhill, to Blackrock, Seapoint, Monkstown, that's the way. Just keep on walking, pass by the puppet theatre – 'night, 'night, puppets, all asleep now – and on to Dun Laoghaire harbour.

A sudden low hum scares me for a second and then I realise it's the DART train coming, its ticker-tack of light flashing by me. In the darkness the sea is lapping in, clawing the sandcastles, filling in the pawmarks, footprints and scattered bits of rubbish left on the damp, cold sand.

Part of me is real proud. I never thought that I could walk this far. It must be miles. Bet they miss me at home. Bet they are starting to worry. Let them!

Missing

GREG – *Monday*

'Conor! Get down here at once! The tea is ready!' I shout up at him again. If that creep wants his meal cold, that's his decision.

Dad is in good form. He got a long letter from Mum in the post this morning and he's going for a drink in the golf club tonight with three of the guys he works with.

'Grace, run up and tell Conor to come down!' Dad tells her.

'Not there,' she announces, shaking her head and waggling her two skinny, crooked plaits. Conor is always late or last in. Dad opens the back door and roars out his name. Sometimes it works, if Conor is hanging round the garden or the road.

'He never misses it! He knows I'm going out tonight and that I want to get his homework checked after tea,' Dad fumes.

•   •   •

Conor still has not turned up. Lucy tidies up, even though it is his turn to pack the dishwasher today. Dad sends me off on a wild-goose chase to a few of the neighbours, in case he has gone into one of their houses, and forgotten the time. No such luck!

'Which of his friends would he be with?' Dad demands, pacing up and down and getting more annoyed.

I can't make any suggestions. He hasn't got a lot of friends, the kid's a loner.

'Dad, he might be in his club, you know with that guy John,' Lucy offers.

'That's it! That's where he probably is. I'll kill him when I get my hands on him!'

Dad gives it about another forty minutes, then he and Lucy head off in the car to John's house. None of us can remember his Dad's name, but Lucy thinks she knows the house.

Conor's not there. His friend said there was some kind of row and that none of them has seen him for hours. Dad is furious, shouting at the three of us: 'Phone this!' 'Get that!' 'Do you know this?' as if we are to blame for what Conor does.

'Bet he's run away,' Grace announces. I manage to clap my hand over her mouth before she gets a chance to say what I know is coming next: Just like Mum.

Dad slumps on the chair. If Lucy or I said that he would have exploded, but Gracey with those big blue eyes – he nods, just accepting another family calamity.

The Big Search

GRACE – Monday

Dad is really cross about Conor. He phoned the Guards to tell them that Conor was missing, and a Garda car came to our house. There were two Guards, a man and a woman. They wrote down everything Dad said, and they asked him about Mum. They went upstairs to Conor's bedroom and Dad told them what clothes he was wearing.

They asked me all about him and if he ran away often. Everybody is searching for him.

Lucy and Granny keep on crying and saying all kinds of bad things that might have happened to him.

I wish we had a dog. If we had a pet dog, I would

get him to sniff some of Conor's clothes and then track him down.

Dad says I am to stay with Granny and Lucy and not to budge.

I wonder is Conor gone to find Mummy and bring her back?

The Long Hike

CONOR – *Monday Night*

Kingstown – that's what they used to call Dun Laoghaire in the old days. I, Conor Dolphin, made it. I walked all this way, miles and miles.

'The King of Kingstown has arrived,' I shout across the watery blackness of the coast.

The big car-ferry is docked, all lit up like a cruise liner you'd see in a film. The hatch is down, like a huge open mouth for the cars to drive into. Crowds of people are making their way onto it and others are standing at the ticket office. Down below, cars and motorbikes, vans and lorries and container trucks all wait their turn, revving their engines. Lucky people going on holiday. One car has floral wreaths spread all over the back seat – I guess they're going to a funeral. Wouldn't it be great if I could stow away? Then by tomorrow morning I would be in Holyhead, gone from Ireland.

I saunter down to the office, hoping there's some way that I can slip through. If only I could spot a family, then maybe I could pretend to be one of their kids. I notice a hopeful, a guy in a brown corduroy jacket, and he has a kind of file with tickets and papers in it, which the girl behind the glass is checking. He's asking her about cabins. His wife is pushing a baby in a rainbow-striped buggy up and down while guarding their luggage, and a little girl with a mop of red curls and freckles who looks about four is running around her. I wander up and stand close to her, and it looks like we're playing a game. People might think that we're brother and sister.

'Honey! We got a four-berth with a shower,' the man calls.

She wheels the buggy towards him and the little girl rushes past me. I smile and try to follow, but the Dad turns back, swoops down and grabs the luggage, then urges them forward and blocks me as he goes through the turnstile. Anyone can see I'm not part of this family.

It's easy enough to mosey up and down the line, but I just can't find a way of getting on the boat. Maybe tomorrow will be better. I can get my money out of the post office and buy a ticket and follow someone on board.

Soon there are no passengers left. The girl behind the glass smiles at me and she whispers something to a man in a navy uniform. I take to my heels and get away.

It's getting cold. The night sea air is chilly and I can feel it through my jacket. My feet are hurting me – the middle part of my foot is sore, and the big toe-nail is pushing out in my old trainers. Up on the roadway, a white van is selling hot dogs and chips, the smell of frying and onions fills the air and makes me realise how starving I am.

'One of each, please!' It takes about half my cash. I ask the lady for a cup of water too. She looks at me and, I guess, realises that I haven't enough money for a can. She reaches behind her and lifts a can of orange off the shelf, gets two plastic cups and divides the sparkling orange between them. She is hot and sweaty from cooking, and takes a long gulp of the drink, then she shoves the other cup towards me.

'Go on! Take it! I'd never finish a whole can and it would only go flat.'

'Thank you! Thank you very much,' I mutter.

I move out of the way of her other customers, sit down on a wooden seat, and wolf the food down. My stomach is rumbling with hunger and is not used to eating so late. I sip the orange slowly, trying to make it last. The plastic cup I save and put in my bag.

Now that I'm fed, I realise I have to get somewhere to sleep the night. If I'd had any sense I would have taken Greg's sleeping bag with me. This seafront bench is too exposed. It might be okay in the summer, but now it's freezing cold.

The shadow of the yacht club sticks out, and I can hear the clanging of the rigging ring out across the harbour. I go down the steps, and walk along by the slip. Beside it there is a sort of dry-dock, and the yard is jammed with yachts and cruisers and dinghies. A high wire mesh protects the yard, and it seems like there is no way in, then in the semi-darkness I spot the almost invisible door in the mesh. My fingers trace around it until I find the lock. It's locked. No, wait! It isn't fully closed. The iron is rusty and stiff from all the salt air. I jiggle it and pull it till it opens and I can squeeze in, and then I re-close the gate.

I can barely see in the darkness. I run my hands along the boat frames, wood and fibreglass, unable to see their names. A few have large canvas covers to protect them.

I must make no noise, I tell myself. Some of the grander yachts may have alarms fitted. I bump into things on every side until I find a boat covered with sort of popper fastenings. I pull them open, climb up and slip in underneath. Some fool has left a tin and a paintbrush on the deck which nearly sends me flying. Up front is a tiny cabin-cum-galley. The mattress has been stored away. Up in the top corner, I open the wooden door and there it is, smelling of salt and sweat, but dry enough. There are life jackets too. I pull one on to keep me warm, another I use as a pillow, and the last I stretch open like a blanket on top of me.

It's kind of scary and stuffy here. Closing my eyes I try to pretend I'm at sea, that I can feel the swell of the waves and the creak of my ship's timbers as we sail to foreign shores.

* * *

'Woof! Woof!' The rough barking noise wakes me and a harsh light is blinding me. 'Quiet, Laddie! Quiet down!'

Some old geezer is standing over me, holding a huge torch and some kind of big stick.

'Don't hurt me, Mister! I've done nothing!' I feel so scared I'm nearly sick.

He motions for me to get up. 'Don't try to run away!' He obviously knows what I'm thinking.

A large golden labrador is standing guard nearby, watching us as we clamber off the boat.

'This way, son!' he says as he leads me into the empty clubhouse. He switches off lights as we pass through a big dining-room with tables set with crisp, white linen cloths, then a bar, its walls adorned with brass anchors and compasses and sailing instruments. The corridor after that is lined with paintings of famous ships and plaques saying the years they were built. The dog wags its tail at me as I follow it along the polished wooden floors. Next comes a huge room with picture windows and a balcony out almost over the water's edge.

'In here!' says the old man.

We go into a small, poky cubby-hole of a room. There are two chairs, one is a large armchair with a rug thrown on it. A bare bulb swings from the ceiling, and the light is so bright compared to outside it almost blinds me.

'Sit down, son!'

The old guy sits down and unzips his big quilted green jacket. He is smaller and frailer than I thought.

'Bernard's the name,' he announces.

I don't tell him mine. He puts his keys and torch on the desk alongside a foil-wrapped packet of sandwiches.

'I'm the night watchman here. My job is to make sure nothing bad happens to this club-house or to the property of its members. I check that the boats are moored okay and not interfered with by vandals. Do you get my meaning?'

I nod. 'I'm not a vandal! Honest, Mr ...'

'Bernard.'

'I just needed somewhere to sleep the night.'

'Where do you live, son?'

Dumb ... just play dumb.

After two or three minutes he knows I won't tell him anything.

'Listen, son! I'm going to have to inform the police about finding you, but before I do, I want to tell you I know what it's like. How old are you? Ten? Eleven? Maybe twelve. I ran away to sea myself when I was a lad of fourteen. Broke my mother's heart I did, but at the time I didn't care a fig about anything like that. Travelled the world I did. Every big port you care to name, I sailed to them all. Scrubbed the decks, waited on the passengers, washed the dishes, odd jobs in the engine room, oh I had adventures, no doubt about it! Never officer material, but still, I got to see all the sights they saw – jungles, beautiful islands, them pyramids, volcanoes, Greek temples, the Arctic with icebergs, the lot. Then I decided to come home, see the family. But I was a stranger to them, and my brothers and sisters had moved all over the place. My mother was older. Truth is, we didn't have a lot to say to each other. So I left and sailed again. Lived in Australia for five years, then moved again. Now I'm retired, I have a flat out Sandycove way, and a small pension. Never was a saver. I should be surrounded by my family and grandchildren, but instead I'm on my own, down here at night minding other people's boats. Laddie, here, is my best mate.'

The old dog ambles over to him and rests a big golden paw on his lap.

'Been a runaway, been a stowaway,' he mumbles, staring at me for reaction. 'So you could say I know what I'm talking about.'

I consider his words carefully. I don't know this man, and he doesn't know me. But he had guessed what I was going to try and do.

The phone lies on the table between us. Will he phone the Guards? I'm not sure.

'What about your Mam and Dad?' he questions, unwrapping the brown bread and ham sandwiches, sharing a bit with me and passing a corner to the dog.

'My Mum and Dad have split up.'

'Oh! Divorced.'

'No! My Mum went to England ... took off and left us ... it's a trial separation.'

'Were you going to go and try to find her and bring her back?'

'I don't know.'

'It's always hard to go back. Takes a brave man,

or woman for that matter. Still and all, son, your Dad'll be worried, your family, your Mam too!' He nods in the direction of the phone.

'No, Bernard.' I shake my head.

He munches on a crust of brown bread, then begins to fold up the foil and the crumbs, moving slowly. He plugs in an electric kettle in the corner, then sits watching me. 'Will I phone for you?'

I nod and tell him the number. The phone clicks and rings.

It's answered straight away. 'DAD!' I can hear my sister shouting ...

Big Trouble

GRACE – Monday Night

Dad went out in the car again in the middle of the night.

Conor is found.

Granny made us all kneel down and say a prayer to say 'Thank you' to God for his safe return.

I am glad, 'cos I love Conor. Sometimes he's funny and he tells me jokes he heard in school. He gives me conkers and shells and stones and sweets ... sometimes.

Greg says he is going to give him hell when he sees him.

Lucy says that Conor is in the biggest, worstest trouble of his whole life for all the trouble and upset he has caused.

Poor Conor!

Prodigal Son

CONOR – *Monday Night*

'Here's the lifejacket, Bernard.' I take it off and hand it back to him.

'No harm done, son! I'll put it back in the morning when it's brighter, before I knock off work.'

Dad is studying the brass name-list of club presidents screwed on the wall. 'We appreciate very much all you've done, Mr ... eh ... Bernard.' Dad is embarrassed.

'As I said, Mr Dolphin, no harm done. He's a good lad. Bit of spirit – bit of courage! Things get to boys that age.'

Bernard walks us to the club-house door. Dad is parked right outside.

'A few hours' sleep, Conor, and you'll feel a new man,' Bernard tells me, shaking my hand. 'Go easy on the lad!' I hear him whisper to Dad just before he gets into the car.

I watch the old sailor and his dog disappear back into the yacht club.

This has got to be the longest drive ever. Dad looks like he could strangle the steering wheel.

'Dad! I'm sorry!'

He won't answer, just keeps on driving, headlights full-on. The roads are deserted and an ambulance, with sirens and lights flashing, screams past us.

'Conor! Never, *ever* do anything like this to me again!'

He takes a half-swipe at me ... his fist punching against my shoulder. The shock and pain rush up my neck, across my back and down my shoulder.

Dad does not look at me. His face is real white, and a blue-coloured vein is pulsing up and down on his neck.

Never, ever again we both promise ... silently.

Stocktaking

GREG – *Thursday*

'How's it going, Dad?' I ask a few nights later. He's poring over a pile of papers spread all over the kitchen table.

'Not too good!' He scratches the stubble on his chin. 'I'm way down this month. Just wait till the accounts section compare it with the figures for this time last year.'

'Are people just not buying, is that it?'

'No, Greg! I'm not out there selling enough. Take this new horse antibiotic. I pleaded with them to advertise and promote it more. Make the vets and trainers and owners more aware of its value to a sick thoroughbred animal. It's damned expensive, but then, you're dealing with valuable racehorse stock. Instead, I'm expected to spend ages trying to interest very busy people in a product they have barely heard of! And I've had so much time off lately ...'

'It's a tough job selling, isn't it?'

'For sure! That's what your Mum says!'

'Did you ever think of changing jobs?' I ask, curious.

'For God's sake, Greg! Don't you start on at me, the way your mother used to!'

'I only meant it might be easier for you –'

'I've been a medical rep all my working life, it's what I know. Your mother got a bee in her bonnet about me changing direction a few months ago. Old man Costigan was retiring and she wanted me to go for his job. It's a desk job and I'd be doing the figures all the time back in the office. No travelling. I'd never meet anyone and I just didn't want to do it. I like meeting the farmers and the vets when I'm on the road. Vanessa's been brooding about it ever since. Maybe that's why ... you see, she thought I could spend more time at home ...'

He starts to stab at the calculator, punching in figures and ignoring me.

'Dad! Did you phone Mum back?'

He keeps on writing down more figures.

'You know she phoned today and wanted to talk to you.'

'I'll do it tomorrow –'

'You are so thick! Don't you *want* her to come back?'

'Greg, this is none of your business!'

'It *is* my business if my parents break up and my whole family is messed up. You should have gone to London after her, brought her back, sorted things out.'

'Maybe ...'

'That's what *I'd* do.'

'Well, that's you!'

'Yeah! You're just pathetic. Why don't you fight for what you want?'

'That's enough, Greg!'

I mean it. My Dad is so stubborn. Well, *he* may be willing to let things slip away, but *I* won't. I'm going to write to Mum and tell her the shambles he's in trying to be a good father and mother too at the moment, and that she has got to come home. Running away is no solution. Dad needs her as much as we do.

Finding a Job

GREG – *Saturday*

Finding a part-time job isn't half as easy as I thought it would be. I tried all the local pubs and they all have plenty of staff. They said to try again next year when I'm a bit older. One guy said he might consider me as a washer-upper, but one look at those big greasy pots and pans made my stomach turn.

The supermarket has a waiting list of trolley attendants and shelf stackers. They said maybe around next Christmas they might need extra staff.

If I had enough money I would consider investing in a big motor mower and go round cutting grass, but they cost a fortune. Then I decided to try the garden centre where Mum and Dad go sometimes.

Mr Murray asked me all kinds of questions about plants and flowers and shrubs, and I think he copped on fairly quickly that I hadn't a clue. Then he asked me what sports I play in school. He's a bit of a rugby fanatic himself. His brother got capped for Ireland years ago.

'I think we'll have to find a job around the place

for a decent lad like yourself,' he said finally.

I still can't believe it, I got a job. I have to help the housewives and old dears out to their cars with their plants and pots and huge bags of moss peat and garden mulch on Saturday and Sunday afternoons, from now till the autumn. The money isn't bad and if they are extra busy I get a bonus.

Dad and Lucy are delighted. Lucy gave me a big hug when I told her after tea. Dad didn't say much, but I know he's proud of me. Conor is dead jealous. When I get my first money next week, I'm going to get some kind of treat for everyone ... even him!

Flying Visit

LUCY – *Saturday*

Dad went to London today. It was only for the day and he got the early-morning flight from Dublin.

Greg says that it's because of him that Dad went. I don't care what the reason is, I'm just glad that he's going to try and talk to Mum. We're all keeping our fingers crossed that he and Mum make up and get back together again.

The day just seemed to drag by, and it was really boring just sitting and watching TV in Deirdre's house. She gave us lasagne and chips for dinner, and we came home at seven o'clock.

All this waiting, not knowing what's going on, is awful, and every time we hear a car turn into the road Greg and I peep out the window to see if it's Dad. Grace doesn't know anything about it as Dad said there was no point in getting her hopes up, and confusing her even more.

It's dead late by the time Dad arrives home, and Conor and Grace are sound asleep. Greg and I are bursting with curiosity.

'What happened?' we demand in unison.

'Give me a chance to get my breath back,' begs Dad, throwing off his clothes and putting on his dressing-gown and slippers, 'and Greg, make me a cup of coffee, will you please?'

He sips the coffee slowly, and I can see that he's trying to work out what to tell us.

'Did you see Mum, Dad?' asks Greg.

'Of course I did! We spent the whole day together, we walked and talked, we had lunch, we walked and talked more. To be honest, I think I'm all talked out.'

'What did Mum say?' I plead.

'Firstly, your Mum misses you all terribly, she carries that photo of the four of you everywhere with her. She hated leaving, but she says that she needed to be apart from me so she could think straight. Vanessa feels our lives need to change, that we must think about what kind of family we want to be. The way things had become was eating away at her. She felt that I had opted out of family life, and that she was already like a single parent raising you all on her own ... she said if things are going to stay that way, then she would prefer to make it official, and go through the courts and get custody of all of you.' Dad delivers all this as calmly as he can.

Greg and I say nothing. Actually, I'm really shocked and sad. I can't think of anything to say.

'Maybe she's right. Obviously, I have to make decisions about trying to balance my job and my family. Sometimes it all just seems impossible. Your Mum says that she would like to study or do some kind of course, and then try to get some work. Then she could bring in some money, and there wouldn't be as much pressure on me.'

'That sounds like a good idea,' says Greg.

Dad gives a huge yawn. 'Yeah. Actually, she started a basic computer course in London; Aunt Mary organised it for her. Look, I'm tired,' he says. 'We all have a lot to think about, but it's about time we got some sleep tonight.'

Custody! It's a frightening word. Dad said Mum would get custody of us. Why is it that when parents fight the kids have got to choose which one they are up for, which one they love the most? I remember years ago in school we did a Bible story about about two women who each claimed to be the mother of a new baby. They were brought before the king and he said he would be totally fair and share the baby equally. He raised his sword and was going to cut the poor baby in half. Then one of the women shouted and said: "Let the other woman have the child. I do not want my baby harmed!" Then the wise king knew she was the real mother and handed her back the child. At the moment I feel a bit like that Bible baby, with a big sword hanging over me. I love my Mum and I love my Dad too. I couldn't choose between them. I feel split apart, sliced down the middle.

Second Chance

CONOR – *Tuesday*

Dad has to sit and queue just like all the other parents at the parent-teacher meeting. Mostly it's all mothers.

Philip's Dad is here because his Mum is in hospital after having his new baby sister. Miss Boland calls the parents, one by one, into a small room to talk to them privately.

Our classroom has our projects and art-and-craft work all laid out. I made a brown dinosaur in a swamp out of clay, but a bit of his back leg has broken and fallen off, so some people are not sure what he is. We have to stay in the classroom to show off our stuff while Miss Boland talks to each parent.

John's Mum takes ages but comes out smiling. Dad hates waiting and is trying to look relaxed and read the newspaper until his turn comes.

Here goes! I time how long he's in.

Twelve minutes! How many good or bad things can a teacher tell a parent in that space of time? Dad shakes Miss Boland's hand when he comes out the door. He is standing very tall and straight and I can tell he's not too happy.

*　　　*　　　*

'Not achieving your full potential, Conor! That's what the woman said!'

I glance out the car window.

'Not concentrating! In a dream world! Homework not done! Fighting with his schoolmates! Conor! Look at me when I'm talking to you.'

Dad's face is strained and worried, not cross or angry like I expected.

'I'm sorry, Dad.'

'It's not your fault, Conor. Things at home can't have helped matters. You should have told me how far behind you were in your books.'

'I tried to, Dad!'

'I know – I probably should have helped you more.'

'Mum used to help me ... she understood! You, you don't understand anything. The other kids laugh at me and call me names because I can't do my reading. You've done enough – it's because of *you* Mum walked out!'

Dad slows the car, pulls off the road and parks outside somebody's driveway.

'Conor, we need to get something straight. Your mother left because she was depressed, confused, angry and needed time to think. She left. I stayed. I'm here, doing the best I can. I know it hurts like hell, but for God's sake don't let it destroy you.' Dad grips my arm so tight it forces me to meet his eyes. 'You may have trouble with reading, Conor, but you're intelligent and bright.'

'Who says so?'

'I say so! And so does your teacher!'

'Huh!'

'She feels – we both feel – that you need some remedial teaching at this stage, one-to-one.'

Dad is waiting for me to throw a tantrum, to shout and object. Mum and I talked about this, so I guess I was almost expecting it. I say nothing. Dad slumps on the car wheel with relief.

'You'll go?'

I nod. I know I need to go. Anyway, Mr Donovan, the special teacher, is meant to be okay.

'Miss Boland also told me that you're a fine athlete, brilliant at running, and that your mind is equally sharp and quick. She seems to know you well.'

'I suppose so.'

'Conor! I can't blame you for being angry with me. I hardly know you, I know that now. But I have been trying. You are my son, and I love you.'

What do I say? Tell him: Buzz off! Drop dead! Get lost! Leave me alone! I want to shout those things at him and open the car door and run, but something makes me hold back.

He leans forward as if blocking my escape plan.

I barely nod.

'You'll give your poor old Dad a second chance, then?'

Two nods.

'Is this a new code?' He begins to laugh. Starting the engine, he honks the horn three times. 'That's Yes in my code, Conor,' he jokes, taking off.

The Dolphin Trail

LUCY – *Wednesday*

Dad has to go to Kerry for a few days. His boss says he has to visit his sales area or they'll transfer it to one of the other reps. We have to go with him as Gran is going to Donegal on her painting holiday and there's no one to mind us.

'Kerry! For heaven's sake! That's miles away,' groans Greg. 'I've to be here for my job.'

'Surely you can start next week, Greg?'

'I'm not going!' Trust Conor. 'My club are all going to the cinema. I don't want to miss it,' he whines.

'Conor, whatever is on in the cinema will probably still be on when we get back,' Dad tries to tell him.

'But I want to go with the rest of them. Next week is no good.'

'Conor, will I ever be able to do or say anything that will please you?' Dad demands angrily.

Perhaps it *would* be nice to get away. Fresh air, open spaces, away from this lonesome house and this road. Yeah, I want to go.

'You've never come with me on any of my trips,' says Dad. 'It will be a nice change.'

'Are we going on our holidays?' Grace asks.

'A little holiday, pet,' Dad says. 'It's not only because your grandmother is going away – I happen to think a few days' break will do us all good.'

'Where will we stay?' I ask.

'We'll stay where I always stay, with Mrs Cooney.'

I can tell Dad is getting excited about the idea. He really wants to take us away with him. He actually likes being with us now.

* * *

Aunt Mary phones from London. She keeps on asking me about Dad, and do we miss Mum, and does *he* miss her. I tell her that he's lonely.

'Lucy, don't you fret or worry,' she says, 'marriages often have a way of being patched up.' Her voice seems distant and far away. She's phoning from her office. She's an architect. Mum always used to say that she was brave and independent enough to make a decent career for herself.

Dad talks to her for ages and ages. 'Your aunt is concerned; she's a good, kind woman,' Dad tells me.

* * *

Grace and I have to share a holdall bag. Dad wants us to take as little as possible. Grace has already managed to stuff it half-full with toys and junk. I'll bring my jeans and togs and a sweater and a few books to read. I hope Kerry is nice. I check to see that Grace has actually got some clothes in.

*   *   *

'Dad! The phone!'

It's Aunt Mary again! My aunt is almost shouting down the line at him. I hang around, hoping he'll tell me about it. Whatever it is, it must be really important!

Dad puts down the phone. He looks like a person who might have won the lottery, but doubts that he filled in the numbers properly.

He turns his back in order to avoid my stare. He doesn't want me to see his face. I know he's hiding something.

At six o'clock we are all sitting down having shepherd's pie – the potato is a bit soggy and the meat is a bit dry. Grace only wants the top potato bit, and Conor only wants the meat bit. I am trying to separate it for them.

'I have news!' Dad is playing with his food, making

a zig-zag with his fork. 'Your mum ... is ... is coming back.'

Well! Talk about a stunned silence! It feels like we're in some kind of weird time-warp in our kitchen.

'Oh Dad! That's great!' Greg is clapping Dad on the back as if *he* has done something marvellous. 'When is she coming home?' he asks.

Dad just shrugs his shoulders. 'I'm not sure yet. Maybe soon.'

'My Mummy is coming home, my Mummy is coming home!' Grace hops up from the table and does some kind of strange, happy dance around the kitchen.

Dad is looking at me for my reaction. Deep inside I feel that the clenched hand that has had a grip on my heart for the last few weeks has loosened its fingers and a rush of relief is flooding my body. Yet, there is some kind of wariness there. 'Oh, Dad, that's the best news I ever heard. It's just too good to be true.' Like a big baby I feel like crying. Mum will be back sitting at the table, talking to us, sorting out Grace and Conor. I just can't wait.

'Is she coming home for good?' asks Conor.

His words startle us.

'Don't be so stupid!' snaps Greg. 'Of course she is!' and he gives Conor a dig in the ribs.

'Stop that, Greg!' warns Dad. 'To be honest, we'll just have to take things slowly. Your Aunt Mary phoned to tell me that your mother has definitely booked a flight to Dublin. I'm sorry, but that's all that I know for the moment.'

'So!' says Conor.

'So?' We all ask him.

'So ... we don't know if Mum is coming home, or if she's just going to come and visit us,' he says.

'Daddy! Daddy! Can we get Mummy a cake?' Grace pleads, climbing up on to Dad's lap.

'Grace, it's not her birthday!' he says softly.

'A pink icey cake – *please*!'

'Maybe we should have a party, a welcome home party. Make welcome home signs,' suggests Greg, all excited too.

'Listen, hold your horses, Greg!' Dad warns. 'Nothing is certain yet. Vanessa and I have a lot to talk about. You must try and allow us the time.' Sometimes I pity my Dad, I think he is almost as unsure as we are.

'No cake! No party! No flags and banners!' Conor puts in. A little blue vein on his right eyebrow throbs – it always does when he's upset. 'She might not stay.'

Grace is glaring at Conor. Her lip is getting wobbly, and I can tell that she's torn between crying and kicking him.

'And ...' he continues, 'and, if she does come back ... well ... maybe she'll leave again.'

Conor waits for Dad to say something. Dad is trying to figure out what to say.

'No cake!' pouts Grace.

'No cake! No promises! No guarantees!' says Dad. 'I'm not a magician. I can't wave a magic wand and turn time back, and pretend none of this has happened. I wish I could, but I just can't. We'll have to make new arrangements. It won't be easy.'

'What about the trip to Kerry?' Greg asks hesitantly.

Suddenly we all remember that our bags are packed and ready to go.

'I have meetings set up. I'd have to cancel them. To be honest, I don't know if the company will put up with me cancelling any more sales trips.' Dad is in two minds about what is the right thing to do. But he has no choice. He mustn't lose his job.

'But what about Mum?' asks Greg, voicing all our thoughts.

Dad stares at the floor. 'Your Mum ... may or may not be back in the next few days. We don't know when.'

'Shouldn't we phone her to tell her about Kerry?' I ask.

In my mind I can picture Mum arriving and opening the hall door, turning the key and stepping inside, and all of us there laughing and happy and pretending it didn't matter. A part of me wants to sit inside that hall door, waiting and waiting, but the other part of me wants her to open the door and step inside and find that I'm gone, that we're all gone, just so she'll know what it feels like. I want to punish Mum – but am I being fair, I wonder?

'We should go to Kerry!' Conor is adamant. 'Do we want to spend the next few days watching the path outside, waiting for the key in the door, waiting for the phone to ring?'

'Can we get a cake for us when we are on holidays?' begs Grace, making us all giggle.

'All right. Maybe we should go.' Dad shrugs, uncertain. 'I don't want to phone her, make her feel pushed. Better if she comes in her own good time.'

'Why don't we leave her a letter?'

Trust Conor. She did that when she left – that's what we're all thinking.

Dad begins to laugh. He laughs and laughs. He laughs so hard he nearly cries.

The Painting

GRACE – *Wednesday*

This new painting is too wet and a bit messy. I forgot to clean my brush since the last time and bits of purple have blobbed in my painting.

Lucy is cross and says that I'm not let bring any more toys in my backpack. She says that I have far too much stuff and takes some things out, but I sneak them back in when she's not looking. We're all going on a holiday with Daddy. I wish Mummy was coming too. It's a big journey and I hope I don't get car sick like the time we went to Galway.

This time I'm going to Kerry.

I'm going to see the dolphin.

This painting is for Mummy.

Dear Mum

CONOR – *Wednesday*

Dear Mum,

If you read this letter it means that you are back home.

We all miss you, especially me.

I thought I would die when you went to London. I was so sad and lonely, I tried to run away too.

Dad and Gran and Miss Boland and Greg and Lucy all tried to help me but they weren't you. I had to learn to be strong for myself. We have all changed.

Dad is home a lot more now. He is taking us to Dingle for a few days to stay in a farmhouse.

I hope you and Dad are going to stay together. I want us all to be together.

I love you.

Conor.

The Map

GREG – *Thursday*

Kerry is almost two hundred miles from Dublin, about as far as you can go because of the Atlantic ocean. My geography book has lots of information and a map, and in the photos the place looks kind of interesting.

When we slam our front door and get in the car, I hope we're not slamming the door on our family's future.

Once we quit the city, Dad relaxes as we move out onto the open road and the motorway. Dad is used to driving on these roads on his own and automatically switches on the radio for company, forgetting that the four of us are there.

Conor stares out the window. Blink, blink, blink – he's at that nervous twitching again.

Lucy is telling Grace the story of Fungi, the friendly Kerry dolphin, who lives offshore beyond Dingle. Grace is snuggled up beside her and is yawning already. Any kind of journey and that kid drops off to sleep. Forget the scenery and sights along the way, she just conks out.

The road widens and cuts through the green countryside. Fields and more fields speed by. This year, Dad says, the crops will be good and the farmers will be happy. Dad gives me a big long talk about the state of Irish agriculture and he has a load of statistics at his fingertips. I'm quite impressed.

It begins to drizzle. People say it never stops raining in Kerry. Luckily we have our boots and rainjackets and Dad's big golf umbrella.

The car is misting up, the wipers swish back and forth – blink, blink, blink, just like Conor!

Cooneys' Farm

LUCY – *Thursday*

Mrs Cooney's farm guesthouse is just great. It's about a mile outside Dingle and from the upstairs window you have a clear view of the ocean.

Grace and I have a small, neat room with bunk beds. Dad and the boys are in together. The ceilings are so low that Greg has managed to whack his head twice off the wooden beam on the landing already.

'Mind your head!' Dad keeps shouting at him.

There are lots of little steps up and down all over the place, and narrow corridors. It's like a rabbit warren. Grace and Conor are chasing around, exploring.

Downstairs, there is a lovely waxy smell of polish and the aroma of the roast lamb Mrs Cooney is cooking for our dinner.

'Something good after your long journey,' she told us all when we arrived.

It was a long drive, but the minute we saw the coast road, and the Cooneys' whitewashed house with all its shining windows winking in the sunlight, and the heather-covered hills sheltering the farm and its buildings, we knew it was worth it.

Dad and Mrs Cooney are old friends, as he has stayed here before, and she made us very welcome when Dad introduced us one by one.

Dad and herself chat away over a cup of tea.

'Dad! Can we go outside?' pleads Conor.

'Okay! But put your boots on,' Dad warns.

Outside it's still very damp but the fresh air helps to wake us up.

The farm is huge. There is a small orchard at the side of the house, and the apple trees are old and wizened. We squash the rotten windfall apples that have been lying for months on the ground, squelching them with our boots. The plum and cherry trees still have dotted clumps of blossom on them. In the late summer there will be raspberries and gooseberries too. I'd like to see it in the summer.

Beside the front door there is a wrought-iron bench, and we all take turns sitting on it. It overlooks the lawn and a straggly path which leads to a goldfish pond, almost completely overgrown with lily pads and pondweed.

Grace almost falls in, bending down to see if there are any goldfish.

We walk through one or two fields, clambering over fences. None of us dares go into the one with all the cows.

'Dinner!' calls Dad.

We all want to stay out. 'Ten more minutes,' we beg. 'We want to explore. It's not dark yet.'

Nothing will make him change his mind. 'No, kids! Tomorrow's another day!'

One thing we do know is that our Dad is as

stubborn as a donkey, and he hates changing his mind. Anyway, we're all starving!

*   *   *

The very minute breakfast is over this morning, Dad sets off to do his business calls. 'Greg is in charge,' he tells us, 'and Mrs Cooney is in charge of Greg!'

Honest to God, this is the best place I ever stayed in. I bet there are ghosts and treasure and secret passages in an old house like this. Grace loves the window-seat in the livingroom, and she keeps pulling the curtains and hiding there. She thinks because she can't see us, that must mean we can't see her!

All morning we have to stay inside as it's lashing rain outside, and a heavy mist is wrapped around the house so that we can barely see to the road. But by lunchtime it has cleared to a drizzle.

'That's what keeps the countryside looking so green,' Mrs Cooney tells us. 'Away off with ye now! A good soft rain never did anyone a bit of harm.'

Greg makes us put on our raincoats and boots and pull up our hoods. Mrs Cooney looks at us as if we're sissy city kids as we set off to explore. Grace is being such a drag that Greg has to pull her along. Dad is whistling by the time he gets back. That's a good sign. It means that he has done really well.

On Saturday morning the rain has moved off and the sky has cleared and we all want to go into Dingle and see it for ourselves. Dad gives us pocket-money, so we can buy something.

Dingle is a busy little town, real picture-postcard stuff. Two Germans take a photo of Conor and me looking in the bookshop window. We pretend not to notice their camera. There are lots of cottages and brightly-painted buildings and craftshops. Dad buys us each an ice-cream and we eat it as we walk about. We get a bag of doughnuts in the bakery shop for later. Greg buys a book about Kerry with lots of beautiful colour pictures. In the craftshop there is a round stand with brooches on it. They look beautiful against the black velvet. There's one of a cat who looks a lot like Max, only thinner, basking in the sun and sitting on a pile of daisies. I buy it for Gran. I want one for myself, but I can't make up my mind which to choose. There's an Irish cottage, lots of different cats, a fishing boat, and dolphins – blue, grey, black and white – one of them is kind of smiling and looks like it's jumping through the waves. That's the brooch for me. I pin it on my yellow jumper.

Grace gets a new bucket and spade, and an inflatable blue ball. Conor is so weird. He wants a kind of dark wooden carving, made from bog oak, of a man leaning against a boat – well, part of one.

'Are you sure?' Dad asks, puzzled.

'Yep!' says Conor.

'Wouldn't you prefer a book or a game?'

'No, Dad! I like this,' Conor says, holding it.

Dad ruffles his hair and pays the man in the shop for it. Wouldn't you know it, Conor's costs more than everyone else's.

'All the shopping done? All the money gone? Then let's head for the most beautiful beach in the country!' Dad announces.

The beach *is* beautiful, breathtaking and bleak. A bracing wind that catches my hair and stings my cheeks blows in off the Atlantic. The ocean stretches out in front of us so that it is hard to tell where the blue of the sky ends and the sea starts. The waves roll in, one after another, splashing on to the cool, golden sand. Miles out, the sea is calm and gentle. Bits of rock jut up, and black glistening cormorants dive from them, then reappear in the swell of water that swirls and tosses against the unmoving ruggedness of the rocks.

Dad takes off his jacket, folds it, and sits down on the sand.

'Can we go for a paddle?' begs Grace, already pulling off her boots and socks.

'It's a bit cold yet, Gracie. The water hasn't had a chance to warm up,' Dad says.

'Please! Please, Dad' she cajoles.

We all copy her and take off our things, and roll up our trouser legs. We should have had the sense to bring a towel with us.

The water is so cold that the second you hit it, you almost freeze your toes off, and stop breathing.

'OW! OW! OW!' Conor and Grace are hopping up and down in the water and squealing so loudly you'd think a giant crab had grabbed them by the toes.

'Greg, what are those islands in the distance called?' I ask.

'The Blaskets, I think.'

'We'll look at them in your school map when we get back to the car,' Dad says.

Greg never says a word. The map is in Dublin. I saw it – he left it on his desk, on top of his books, with a big circle drawn around Dingle. Just like I left my diary, half-by-accident and half-on-purpose on my bed, wide open.

'Daddy! Daddy! Look!' Grace is screaming and shouting with excitement.

'I see a dolphin – a *real* dolphin.'

We all stare in the direction she's pointing.

'The dolphin! You must see him,' she insists.

'That's not a dolphin, pet,' Dad reasons. 'Fungi swims much further out than this. You have to go out in a boat to see him.'

'But I *see* him. He's jumping in the waves,' Grace says determinedly.

'I think that's just a bit of rock sticking up out of the seabed,' Dad tells her gently.

Before any of us can stop her, she lurches forward and wades in up to her waist. Greg manages to grab hold of her before she goes any further or falls under.

She's soaking. Her tracksuit bottoms are sodden, so we just pull them off her, leaving her top and knickers on. Her skin is blue and covered in goosepimples. Dad picks up his jacket, shakes the sand off it, and wraps it around her to keep her warm till we get back to the farm.

Usually Grace would be crying her head off by now when something like this happens, but today she clings to Dad, saying smugly: 'I did see a dolphin. I saw a dolphin!'

Comeback

CONOR – *Saturday*

Grace is wild with excitement, talking about the dolphin. Of course none of them believe her. I saw it too – well, I'm almost sure I did. It was watching us. I could sense it.

Only a few more hours and we'll have to leave Dingle and go back to Dublin. I wish we could stay here for ever and ever. Dad is in good humour. He must have sold lots of products and filled his order book. He gave me extra money for my present. For my 'thinking man'.

The beach here is nice but I think that I prefer Brittas Bay. One thing is certain, the sea here is freezing. It's lonesome here no matter how beautiful it is. We're the only kids on the strand.

If I turn my back to the ocean and look, all I can

see is the golden sand with bits of brown stringy seaweed, and sharp grey rocks, then field after green field, all drawn out with low stone walls and scraggy hawthorn hedges. That's what it would look like if I was a fisherman out bobbing on the sea, fixing my nets ... or a big ocean fish, silver blue, jumping in the sea spray.

The ocean, the fields, the hills – I wish they could be mine for ever. No more school, no more home-work, no more living in a sad house. Dad is staring out to sea, maybe he's wishing the very same thing.

'Conor! Grace!' A voice catches on the wind. Someone is calling us.

'Greg! Lucy! Conor! Grace!'

I turn towards the sound. A grey gull screeches through the sky. My eyes skim the distance. I know the voice, her face is nervous. The brown hair is shorter. She stands with her arms thrown wide open.

'MUM!'

I run first. The others turn, curious, and realising what's happening begin to follow. I'm the fastest runner in the world, even if it is on heavy sand and slightly uphill.

'Oh, my Conor!' She closes her arms around me,

and hugs me close to her, till one by one the others crush in on top of us.

'I'm sorry! I'm so sorry for leaving you all!' The way she says it we know that she means it.

Dad walks over slowly to join us and stops in front of Mum. Neither of them says a word. He just takes her hand.

'I saw a dolphin today, Mummy, I really did!' Grace announces.

Mum lifts her up, ignoring how wet and sandy she is, and nuzzles her hair.

'I saw a dolphin too, pet, your dolphin, the one with the purple spots.'

'My painting,' nods Grace.

'I got the letter ...'

My face goes red.

'And I guessed then that I needed to follow the trail.'

'The trail?' asks Dad, confused.

'Yes, Chris, the painting, the letter, the diary, the maps ... the trail that led me all the way to here, where I am meant to be!'

'We have to go back home today, Vanessa,' Dad tells her.

She lets her eyes roam around, taking it all in, makes a disappointed face and gives a little frown.

I want Dad to say something.

'By plane, by train, by bus, by taxi, I've come a long way to find this place, Chris, to find you all,' she says. Her voice is tired. She wants to stay here.

Dad avoids her eyes and kicks at the sand. 'We have to get back home,' he insists stubbornly.

I know what he is telling her.

'One more night, Chris,' she pleads. 'Till tomorrow! Then we'll start all over again.'

'Please, Dad! Please! Please! PLEASE!' we all chorus.

He looks at each of us, and at her, making his mind up. 'Till tomorrow, then! One more night in Mrs Cooney's. And tomorrow we go back home – and start over again,' he agrees.

We shout and scream and roar, frightening the gulls with our happiness, and chase each other along the sand and in and out of the waves, while Mum and Dad watch us.

Tomorrow we start the long journey back home.

Other books by
MARITA CONLON-MCKENNA

The Famine Trilogy
UNDER THE HAWTHORN TREE
Illustrated by Donald Teskey

Eily, Michael and Peggy are left without parents when the Great Famine strikes – how will they survive?
A gripping story of love, loyalty and courage.

Paperback £4.99/$7.95

WILDFLOWER GIRL
Illustrated by Donald Teskey

Peggy, from *Under the Hawthorn Tree*, is now thirteen and must leave Ireland for America. After a terrible journey on board ship, she arrives in Boston. What kind of life will she find there?

Paperback £4.99/£7.95

FIELDS OF HOME
Illustrated by Donald Teskey

The horrors of the Famine are over, and the trilogy continues. In America, Peggy hears the call of the wild west. Back in Ireland, will Michael and Eily ever manage to get fields they can call their own?

Paperback £4.99/$7.95

THE BLUE HORSE

When Traveller Katie's family's caravan burns down they are destitute. She must fit into a new life settled in a house. But will she be accepted?

Paperback £4.50/$7.95

SAFE HARBOUR

Two children are evacuated from the horrors of the London blitz to live in Greystones, Co Wicklow, with a stern grandfather they have never met.

Paperback £4.99/$7.95

AND MARITA'S
LATEST NOVEL

IN DEEP DARK WOOD

When the mysterious Bella Blackwell moves in next door to the Murphy family, no one knows quite what to make of her. Rory doesn't trust her at all, but his sister Mia soon falls under the old woman's spell. Bella tells Mia of a faraway place, a world where dragons and giants and ancient magic still exist, and she asks Mia to become her apprentice and to learn the old ways.

Then the trouble begins ...

Paperback £4.99/$7.95